By the Same Author

*Windows on the World*

*Holiday in a Coma & Love Lasts Three Years: Two Novels*

FR
N

FRÉDÉRIC BEIGBEDER

# A FRENCH NOVEL

TRANSLATED FROM THE FRENCH BY FRANK WYNNE

FOURTH ESTATE • *London*

Fourth Estate
An imprint of HarperCollins*Publishers*
77–85 Fulham Palace Road,
Hammersmith, London W6 8JB
www.4thestate.co.uk

First published in Great Britain by
Fourth Estate 2013



1



A catalogue record for this book is available from the British Library

ISBN 978-0-00-737136-5



Typeset in Sabon LT Std by Palimpsest Book Production Limited,
Falkirk, Stirlingshire

Printed and bound in Great Britain by Clays Ltd, St Ives plc

*For my family*
*and for Priscilla de Laforcade*
*who is a part of it*

# FOREWORD

The greatest quality of this book is undoubtedly its honesty. When a book is as honest as this, it can lead, almost unintentionally, to genuine revelations about what it means to be human – in this respect, literature is still leagues ahead of the sciences. In reading *A French Novel*, we realise that a man's life is divided into two phases: childhood and adulthood, and that it is completely pointless to further refine this analysis. Formerly, there existed a third phase, known as *old age*, which linked the two, when childhood memories flooded back, giving a semblance of unity to a human life. But to enter into old age, one must first accept it, leave life behind and enter into the age of memory. Caught up in desires and in adult plans, the author is not at this stage, and has almost no memory of his childhood.

He does, however, have one, involving shrimping and a beach on the côte Basque. Like Cuvier reconstructing the skeleton of a dinosaur from a single fragment of bone, from this single memory Frédéric Beigbeder reconstructs his whole family history. It is a serious, solid work in which we discover a French family, a relatively harmonious blend of bourgeoisie and aristocracy of staunchly rural stock. A family heroic to the point of lunacy during the First World War, and consequently rather more circumspect when the Second World War breaks out. After 1945 they are gripped by a lively appetite for consumerism, an appetite which after 1968 will extend to a new level, becoming widespread in the sphere of *morals*. A family like many others, most of which belong to the upper classes; but it is the very ordinariness of Beigbeder's family history that makes it compelling, since the whole history of twentieth-century France unfolds before our eyes, related without apparent effort. On first reading, we get a little confused sometimes with all the characters; that is the only thing for which one might criticise the author.

In adolescence, everything changes. Memories flood back, but there are two things basically, two things in particular that linger in the author's memory: the girls he has loved, the books he has read. Is that all there is to life, is that all that remains? It would seem so. And here too,

Beigbeder's honesty is so obvious that we would not think to challenge his conclusions. If it is indeed this and this alone that seems important to him, it's because it truly is. Deep down, the pleasure of autobiography is almost the opposite of that of the novel: far from losing oneself in the author's world, we never forget ourselves when reading an autobiography; we compare ourselves, we connect, we confirm, page after page, our sense of belonging to a common humanity.

I was less interested by the sections about the nights spent in custody for taking cocaine on the public highway. It's curious; I should have empathised, having myself spent a night in prison for an offence almost as stupid (smoking a cigarette on a plane) – and I can confirm that conditions in custody are not exactly comfortable. But the author and his friend the Poet protest a little too much; they mouth off. The portrait of the writer as a boy, a sickly little thing, all chin and ears, doing his best to follow in the footsteps of the big brother he admires, is brief, but it is so powerful that I felt I could sense that child reading over my shoulder through the whole book. In this delinquent episode, something is wrong: the child does not recognise himself in the adult he has become. And this, too, is probably the truth: the child is not father to the man.

There is the child, there is the man; and between the two there is no connection. It is a discomfiting, embarrassing conclusion: we would like to think that there is a certain unity at the core of the human personality; it is an idea we find difficult to let go of; we would like to be able to make a connection.

That connection we immediately make is in the pages the author devotes to his daughter, probably the most beautiful in the book. Because imperceptibly he realises, and we realise with him, that the childhood years his daughter is going through are the only years of true happiness. And that nothing, not even his love for her, will prevent her from stumbling over the same obstacles, from sinking into the same ruts. This increasingly poignant blend of secret sadness and love culminates in the magnificent epilogue, which in itself would justify this book, in which the author teaches his daughter, as his grandfather taught him, the art of skimming stones. In that moment the circle is closed and everything is justified. The stone that skips magically 'six, seven, eight times' across the sea. A victory, albeit limited, against gravity.

Michel Houellebecq

*Like a spring, young children grow*
*Then blossom in a summer*
*Surprised by winter they no longer show*
*What once they were.*

Pierre de Ronsard, '*Ode à Anthoine de Chasteigner*', 1550

# PROLOGUE

I am older than my great-grandfather. Capitaine Thibaud de Chasteigner was thirty-seven years old when he fell during the second battle of Champagne, on 25 September 1915 at 9.15 a.m. between the valley of Suippe and the outskirts of the Argonne forest. I had to pester my mother to find out more; the hero of the family is an unknown soldier. He is buried at the Borie-Petit château, in Dordogne (my uncle's place), but I saw his photograph in the château Vaugoubert (belonging to another uncle): a tall, thin young man in a blue uniform, with cropped fair hair. In his last letter to my great-grandmother, Thibaud says he has no wire-cutters to clear a path to the enemy's lines. He describes the flat, chalky landscape, the incessant rain turning the ground into a muddy swampland, and confides that he has received the order to attack the following morning. He knows he will die; his letter is like a 'snuff movie' – a horror film made using no special effects. At dawn, he fulfilled his duty, singing the '*Chant des Girondins*': 'To die for one's country is the most noble, most enviable destiny!' The men of the 161st Infantry Regiment launched themselves into a hail of bullets; as intended, my great-grandfather and his men were ripped to shreds by the German machine guns and asphyxiated with chlorine gas. It might be said that Thibaud was murdered by his superior officers. He was tall, he was young, he was handsome, and *La France* ordered him to die for her. Or rather – and this gives his fate a curious topicality – *La France* ordered him to commit suicide. Like a Japanese kamikaze or a Palestinian terrorist, this father of four sacrificed himself knowing precisely what he was doing. This descendant of the crusaders was doomed to imitate Jesus Christ: to give his life so that others might live.

I am descended from a gallant knight crucified on the barbed wire of Champagne.

# 1

# CLIPPED WINGS

I had just found out my brother had been made a Chevalier de la Légion d'honneur when I was arrested. The police did not handcuff me straight away; they only did that later, when I was being transferred to the Hôtel-Dieu, and again when I was transferred to prison on the Île de la Cité the following night. The President of the Republic had just written a charming letter to my elder brother, congratulating him on his contribution to the economic dynamism of France: 'You are a perfect example of the sort of capitalism we want: a capitalism of entrepreneurs rather than one of speculators.' On 28 January 2008, at the police station in the 8th arrondissement in Paris, officers in blue uniform, guns and truncheons dangling from their belts, stripped me completely naked in order to search me, confiscated my phone, my watch, my credit card, my money, my keys, my passport, my driving licence, my belt and my scarf, took samples of my saliva and my fingerprints, lifted up my testicles to see whether I had anything stuffed up my arsehole, took front, side and three-quarter photographs of me holding a mugshot placard, before returning me to a cage two metres square, its walls covered with graffiti, dried blood and snot. At the time I did not realise that, a few days later, I would be watching my brother receiving the Légion d'honneur in the Salle des Fêtes of the Élysée Palace, which is not quite so cramped, and that through the picture windows I would watch the leaves of the oak trees in the grounds moving in the wind, as though waving to me, beckoning me to come into the presidential gardens. Lying on a concrete bench at about four o'clock in the morning that dark night, the situation seemed simple to me: God had faith in my brother, and He had abandoned me. How could two people who had been so close as children have had such different fates? I had just been arrested for using class-A drugs on the public highway with a friend. A pickpocket in the next cell hammered on the glass half-heartedly, but regularly enough to keep the rest of the prisoners from getting any sleep. Sleep, in any case, would have been impossible, a utopian dream, since even when the convicts stopped bawling, the police shouted to each other along the gangways at the top of their lungs, as though the prisoners were deaf. The air was pervaded by the smell of sweat, vomit and undercooked microwaved stewed beef with carrots. Time passes very slowly when you don't have a watch and when no one thinks to switch off the flickering strip light on the ceiling. Lying on the filthy concrete floor at my feet, a schizophrenic in an alcoholic coma groaned, snored and farted. It was freezing, but I was burning up. I tried to think of nothing, but it was impossible: when you bang people up in a tiny little cell, their brains work overtime trying in vain to ward off panic; some fall to their knees and beg to be let out, others have a nervous breakdown, try to top themselves, or confess to crimes they didn't commit. I would have given anything for a book or a sleeping pill. But since I had neither, I started writing this book in my head, with no pen, my eyes closed. I hope that this book lets you escape from it all, as it did me that night.

# 2

# LOST GRACE

I do not remember my childhood. No one believes me when I say that. Everyone remembers their past; what's the point of living if you forget your life? I have nothing left of myself: from zero to the age of fifteen, I am confronted by a black hole (as defined in astrophysics: 'a compact mass having a gravitational field so intense that no matter or radiation can escape'). For a long time I believed that this was normal, that others experienced the same amnesia. But whenever I asked, 'Do you remember your childhood?', they would tell me endless stories. I'm ashamed that my autobiography will be written in invisible ink. Why is my childhood not indelible? I feel excluded from the world, because the world has an archaeology and I do not. I have covered my tracks like a criminal on the run. When I mention this disability, my parents roll their eyes to heaven, my family protests, my childhood friends get angry, former girlfriends are tempted to produce photographic evidence.

'You haven't lost your memory, Frédéric. It's just that you don't care about us!'

Amnesiacs are hurtful; their nearest and dearest take them for revisionists, as though forgetting is always a choice. I'm not lying by omission: I rummage through my life as if it were an empty trunk, and I find nothing; I am a wilderness. Sometimes I'll hear people whispering behind my back: 'That guy, I can't quite work him out.' I agree. How is it possible to work someone out when he doesn't know where he comes from? As Gide says in *The Counterfeiters*, I am 'built on piles having neither foundations nor substratum'. The ground gives way beneath my feet, I hover on a cushion of air, I am a bottle adrift on the sea, a Calder mobile. In order to please, I gave up having a backbone, I wanted to blend into the background like Zelig, the human chameleon. To forget one's personality, lose one's memory in order to be loved; to become, the better to charm, that which others wish one to be. In psychiatric terms this is a personality disorder known as 'deficiently centred consciousness'. I am an empty vessel, a life without substance. In my childhood bedroom on rue Monsieur-le-Prince, pinned on one of the walls, I'm told, I had a poster for the film *My Name is Nobody*. I probably identified with the hero.

I have always written stories about men who have no past: the heroes of my books are products of an age of immediacy, cast adrift in a rootless present – transparent inhabitants of a world in which feelings are as short-lived as butterflies, in which forgetfulness is a safeguard against pain. It is possible – I am living proof – to retain only a few scraps of one's childhood, false for the most part, or fashioned after the fact. Such amnesia is encouraged in our society: even the future perfect is on the road to grammatical oblivion. My handicap will soon be a commonplace; my particular case will become the general. Nonetheless, we must accept that it is not usual to develop Alzheimer's symptoms in middle age.

Often I refashion my childhood out of politeness. 'Come on, Frédéric, you must remember?' I nod sagely: 'Oh yes, of course, I collected Panini stickers, I was a Rubettes fan, it's all coming back to me now.' I am terribly sorry to have to confess here: I remember nothing; I am my own imposter. I have no idea where I was between 1965 and 1980; perhaps this is why I am so lost today. I hope there is some secret, some mysterious hex, some magic spell I could discover which would lead me out of this personal labyrinth. If my childhood was not a nightmare, why does my mind keep my memory in a coma?

# 3

# FLASHBACKS OF MYSELF

I was a good boy, who meekly trailed around after his mother in her peregrinations, and squabbled with his elder brother. I am one of the mass of non-problem children. Sometimes, I am gripped by the fear that perhaps I remember nothing because there is nothing worth remembering. My childhood might have been a long string of empty, dreary, dismal days, as monotonous as waves on a beach. And what if I remember all there is to know? What if the opening act of my existence has no vivid moments? A sheltered, cosseted, privileged childhood without a whit of originality or depth – what would I have to complain about? To be spared misfortunes, tragedies, bereavements and accidents is surely a stroke of luck in the making of a man. This book would then be an inquiry into the dull, the futile, a speleological journey into the depths of bourgeois normality, an account of French banality. All happy childhoods are alike; perhaps they do not warrant being remembered. Is it possible to put into words all the phases that a small boy was doomed to experience in Paris during the Sixties and Seventies? I would love to tell the story of how I was merely a deduction in my parents' annual tax returns.

My only hope, as I embark on this diving expedition, is that writing can rekindle memory. Literature remembers what we have forgotten: to write is to read within oneself. Writing reawakens memory; it is possible to write as one might exhume a body. Every writer is a *ghostbuster*, a phantom-hunter. Curious phenomena of involuntary recollection have been observed among a number of famous novelists. Writing possesses a supernatural power. One may start writing a book as though consulting a magus or a marabout. Autobiography exists at the crossroads between Sigmund Freud and the famous astrologer Madame Soleil. In his 1969 article 'What is the Purpose of Writing?', Roland Barthes states that 'writing . . . fulfils a task whose origin is indiscernible'. Might that task be the sudden return of a forgotten past? Proust, his madeleine, his sonata, the two loose paving stones in the courtyard of the Hôtel de

Guermantes which raise him up 'towards the silent heights of memory'? Hmm, so, no pressure then. I'd rather choose a less illustrious but more recent example. In 1975, Georges Perec begins *W, or the Memory of Childhood* with this sentence: 'I have no childhood memories.' His book is filled with them. Something mysterious happens when we close our eyes to summon up the past: memory is like those sake cups offered in some Japanese restaurants, where a naked woman gradually appears at the bottom, and disappears as soon as the cup is drained. I see her, I gaze at her, but the moment I get close, she vanishes: my lost childhood is like that. I pray that some miracle will happen here, that my past will slowly develop in this book like a Polaroid. To quote myself, if I may be so bold – and in an autobiographical text, to try to avoid navel-gazing would be to add absurdity to pretension – this curious phenomenon has already manifested itself. In 2002, while I was writing *Windows on the World*, a scene suddenly appeared from nowhere: a cold winter morning in 1978, I am leaving my mother's apartment to walk to school, my US schoolbag on my back, avoiding stepping on the cracks between paving stones. My mouth spewing plumes of condensation, I am bored to death and have to make an effort of will not to throw myself under the number 84 bus. The chapter closes with this sentence: 'I never escaped that morning.' The following year, the last page of *L'Égoïste romantique* evokes the smell of leather in my father's English cars, which as a boy I found nauseating. Four years later, while writing *Au secours pardon*, I revelled in the memory of a Saturday night spent in my father's duplex apartment, where my slippers and my blushes seduced several Scandinavian models who were listening to Stevie Wonder's orange double album. At the time, I attributed these memories to fictional characters (Oscar and Octave), but no one believed they were made up. I was attempting to talk about my childhood, without really daring to.

After my parents' divorce, my life was cut in two. On one side, maternal moroseness; on the other, paternal hedonism. Sometimes the moods were reversed: the more my mother got back on her feet, the more my father immured himself in silence. My parents' moods: the communicating vessels of my childhood. The word vessel also conjures the image of a ship run aground. I clearly had to build myself on shifting sands. For one parent to be happy, it was better if the other was not. This was not a conscious battle; on the contrary, I never saw the slightest hint of hostility between them, yet this pendulum swing was all the more implacable for the fact that they both kept smiling.

# 4

# VOWELS, CONSONANTS

On 28 January 2008, the evening had started out well: dinner washed down with *grands crus*, then the usual bar crawl through dimly lit watering holes, the shots of coloured flavoured vodkas: liquorice, coconut, strawberry, mint, curaçao, downed in one; the shot glasses, black, white, red, green, blue, the colours of Rimbaud's poem 'Vowels'. Riding along on my moped, I hummed the Pixies' 'Where Is My Mind'. I was dressed up as a schoolboy, wearing suede cowboy boots, with unkempt shoulder-length hair, cloaking my age in my beard and my black raincoat. I have indulged in such nocturnal excesses for more than twenty years; it is my favourite hobby, the sport of grown-ups who refuse to grow up. It's not easy being a child trapped in the body of an amnesiac adult.

In Proust's *Sodom and Gomorrah*, the Marquis de Vaugoubert wants to look 'young, virile and attractive, though he could see and no longer dared to peer into his mirror to inspect the wrinkles solidifying around a face whose many charms he would have wished to preserve'. As you can see, the problem is not new: Proust used the name of the château that belonged to my great-grandfather Thibaud. A mild state of inebriation began to envelop reality, to temper my speed, to make my childish behaviour seem acceptable. A new law had been passed by the republic a month previously forbidding smoking in nightclubs, so a crowd had gathered on the pavement along the avenue Marceau. I was a non-smoker expressing solidarity with the pretty girls in patent-leather pumps who huddled around the proffered cigarette lighters. For a second, their faces were lit like a painting by Georges de la Tour. I was holding a glass in one hand, using the other to cling to friendly shoulders. I kissed the hand of a waitress still waiting for a part in a major motion picture, pulled the hair of the editor of a magazine with no readership. An insomniac generation gathered on Monday nights to stave off the cold, the loneliness, the financial crisis already looming on the horizon – God knows, there's no shortage of excuses to get plastered. There was also an actor who dabbled in art-house cinema, a few out-of-work girls, bouncers both black and white, a singer on his way out and a writer whose first novel I had published. When the latter took out a white wrap and began to tip powder onto the bonnet of the gleaming black Chrysler parked in the access road, no one protested. Flouting the law amused us: we were living in an era of Prohibition, it was time to rebel like Baudelaire and Théophile Gautier, Brett Easton Ellis and Jay McInerney, like Antoine Blondin, who was rescued from a police station by Roger Nimier disguised as a chauffeur. I was meticulously cutting the white crystals with a gold credit card while my writer friend bitched that his mistress was even more jealous than his wife, something that he considered (and as you can imagine, I was nodding vigorously in agreement) an unforgivable lapse of taste, when suddenly a strobing light made me look up. A two-tone car pulled up in front of us. On the doors were strange blue letters underscored by a red stripe. The letter 'P'. Consonant. The letter 'O'. Vowel. The letter 'L'. Consonant. The letter 'I'. Vowel. I thought of that TV game show, *Countdown*. The letter 'C'. Oh, fuck. The letter 'E'. Doubtless these widely spaced letters had some hidden meaning. Someone wanted to warn us of something, but what? A siren began to wail, the blue light whirled as on a dance floor. We both scarpered like rabbits. Rabbits in slim-fitting jackets. Rabbits in ankle boots with slippery soles. Rabbits unaware that in the 8th arrondissement 28 January 2008 was the first day of the hunting season. One of the rabbits had even left his credit card with his thermally moulded name lying on the bonnet of the car, while the other did not even think to throw away the illicit packets hidden in his pockets. This dawn marks the end of my endless youth.

# 5

# FRAGMENTS OF AN ARREST

You are the one I have been searching for all
this time,
in the throbbing vaults, on the dance floors
where I never danced,
amid the forest of people,
beneath the light bridges and the sheets of
skin, at the end of painted toenails hanging
over the end of blazing beds,
in the depths of these eyes that hold no promises,
in the back yards of ramshackle buildings,
among lonely dancers and drunken barmen,
between green rubbish bins and silver
convertibles,
I looked for you among fractured stars and
violet perfumes,
in icy hands and syrupy kisses, at the bottom
of rickety staircases,
at the top of brightly lit elevators,
in pallid joys, in seized opportunities, in fierce
handshakes,

and in the end I had to stop looking for you
under a starless vault,
on white boats,
in downy necklines and dark hotels,
in mauve mornings and ivory skies, among
  marshy dawns,

my vanished childhood.

The police wanted to confirm my identity; I did not protest, it was something I too needed to confirm. 'Who is it that can tell me who I am?' asks Lear in Shakespeare's play.

I haven't slept a wink all night. I don't know whether the day has dawned: my sky is a crackling white fluorescent tube. I am squeezed into a lightbox. Deprived of space and time, I occupy a container of eternity.

A custody cell is the part of France where maximum pain is concentrated into the minimum square footage.

It is impossible to cling to my youth.

I have to dig deep within myself, like the prisoner Michael Scofield digging a tunnel in *Prison Break*. To remember in order to go over the wall.

But how can someone take refuge in memories when he has none?

My childhood is not some paradise lost, nor some ancestral trauma. I imagine it more as a slow period of obedience. People have a tendency to idealise their childhood, but a child is first and foremost a bundle that you feed, carry and put to bed. In exchange for bed and board, the bundle conforms on the whole to policies and procedures.

Those who are nostalgic about their childhood are people who miss the time when they were looked after by others.

In the end, a police station is like a day-care centre: they undress you, feed you, keep an eye on you, stop you from leaving. It's not illogical that my first night in prison should take me back so far.

There are no more adults, only children of all ages. To write a book about my childhood therefore means talking about myself in the present. Peter Pan is amnesiac.

It's curious that we say someone 'saved his own skin' when he runs away. Isn't it possible to save your skin while staying put?

I can taste salt in my mouth, just as I used to at the beach at Cénitz when I accidentally ended up swallowing seawater.

# 6

## GUÉTHARY, 1972

Of my entire childhood, one single image remains: the beach at Cénitz, near Guéthary; Spain barely visible, sketched along the horizon, a blue mirage suffused with light; this would have been around 1972, before they built the purification plant that stinks, before the restaurant and the car park blocked the path down to the sea. I see the image of a scrawny little boy and an emaciated old man walking side by side along the beach. The grandfather is much more dashing, tanned and handsome than his sickly, pale grandson. The white-haired man skims flat stones on the sea; they skip across the water. The little boy is wearing an orange swimsuit with a seashell embroidered on the terrycloth; his nose is bleeding, a wad of cotton wool pokes out of his right nostril. Count Pierre de Chasteigner de la Rocheposay looks very like the actor Jean-Pierre Aumont. He shouts, 'Do you know, Frédéric, I've seen whales, blue dolphins, even an orca, right here?'

'What's an orca?'

'It's a big, black killer whale with teeth as sharp as razorblades.'

'But . . .'

'Don't worry, the monster can't come close to the shore, he's too big; here on the beach you're in no danger.'

To be on the safe side, I decided that day never to set foot in the water again. My grandfather was teaching me to shrimp with a net, and I remember why my elder brother was not with us. At the time, an eminent doctor had told my mother I might have leukaemia. I was on a rest cure, in 'rehab', at the age of seven. I had come to the seaside to gather my strength, to breathe in the fresh salt air through a nose clotted with blood. In my grandfather's house 'Patrakénéa' (Basque for 'The Peculiar House'), in my damp room, a green hot-water bottle would be slipped into my bed; it made a sploshing sound when I moved, and regularly reminded me of its presence by scalding my feet.

The brain twists childhood, to make it better or worse, to make it more interesting than it was. Guéthary 1972 is like a recovered sample of DNA; like the white-coated forensic officer in the 8th arrondissement police station who has just swabbed the insides of my cheeks with a wooden spatula to get a mucus sample, I should be capable of recreating everything from this single strand of hair found on the beach. Unfortunately I am not skilled enough: closing my eyes in my squalid little cell, I can reconstruct only the rocks chafing the soles of my feet, the murmur of the Atlantic roaring in the distance alerting us to the rising tide, the slippery sand between our toes, and my pride that my grandfather has made me responsible for holding the bucket of shrimps wriggling in the brine. On the beach, a few old ladies pull on flowery bathing caps. At low tide, the rocks form little swimming pools, in which the shrimp are held prisoner. 'You see, Frédéric, you have to scrape around inside the fissures. Go ahead, it's your turn.' As he held out the shrimping net, my grandfather, with his white hair and pink espadrilles bought from Garcia, taught me the word 'fissure'; keeping the net close to the jagged edges of the rocks beneath the water, he caught the poor creatures as they jumped backwards into his net. I tried my luck, but caught only a few listless hermit crabs. But it didn't matter: I was alone with Bon Papa, and I felt as heroic as he. Walking back up from Cénitz beach, he picked blackberries along the roadside. It was miraculous for a little city kid holding his grandfather's hand, to discover that nature was a sort of giant smorgasbord: the ocean and the trees teemed with gifts, you had only to stoop and pick them up. Until then I had only ever seen food come out of a fridge or a shopping trolley. I felt as if I were in the Garden of Eden, its pathways burgeoning with fruit.

'One day, we'll go to the woods at Vaugoubert and pick ceps under the fallen leaves.'

We never did.

The sky was an uncharacteristic blue: for once, the weather was fine in Guéthary, and the houses seemed to get whiter as we watched, like in those ads for Ajax: The White Tornado. But perhaps it was overcast, perhaps I'm trying to arrange things, perhaps I just need the sun to shine upon the one memory I have of my childhood.

# 7

# NATURAL HELLS

When the police descended on us on the avenue Marceau, we were a dozen revellers huddled together, lighting cigarettes around a car whose gleaming bonnet was striped with parallel white lines. We were more like Marcel Carné's *Youthful Sinners* than Larry Clark's junkie *Kids*. As soon as the siren began to wail, we scattered to the four winds. The officers only managed to net two delinquents, like my grandfather shrimping, delving into the fissures – in this case the entrance to Alma-Marceau métro station, whose shutters were closed at this late hour. While my friend – let's call him the Poet – was being arrested, I heard him protest, 'Life is a nightmare!' The baffled face of the Policeman in front of the Poet will continue to make me smile until my dying day. Two keepers of the peace carried us right up to the bonnet of contention; I remember having enjoyed this exercise in nocturnal levitation. The ensuing dialogue seemed to be perched midway between Poetry and Public Order.

Policeman: 'What the hell were you thinking, doing something like that on a car?'

Poet: 'Life is a NIGHTMARE!'

Me: 'I am descended from a gallant knight who was crucified on the barbed wire of Champagne.'

Policeman: 'All right, that's it, take this lot down to Sarij 8.'

Me: 'What's Sarij 8?'

Policeman II: 'The service for reception, research and judicial investigation of the 8th arrondissement.'

Poet: '"As human beings advance through life the romance which dazzled the young man, the fabulousss legend which enchanted him as a child, these wither and grow dim of themselvesss . . ."'

Me *(simultaneously brown-nosing and showing off)*: 'That's not his. Surely you must have read Baudelaire's *Artificial Paradises*, Captain? You know that artificial paradises exist to help us escape our natural hells?'

Policeman *(into his radio)*: 'Boss, we've got a violation here!'

Policeman II: 'You're crazy to do this on a public highway! Why don't you hide in the bogs like everyone else? That's provocation, that is!'

Me *(wiping the powder from the bonnet of the car with my scarf)*: 'We are not everyone else, *Commandant*. We're WRRRRITERS. OK?'

Policeman *(brutally grabbing my arm)*: 'Boss, the apprehended individual tried to destroy a piece of evidence!'

Me: 'Hey, hey, easy does it, Mr Officer Sir, no need to break my arm. I liked it better when you carried me.'

Poet *(with vehement head movements intended to express human dignity and the pride of the misunderstood artist)*: 'Liberty is an impossibility . . .'

Policeman: 'Can't you get this guy to shut up?'

Poet *(convinced he is convincing, articulating every syllable, one finger raised like a tramp muttering to himself in the métro)*: 'The Powers That Be need aaartists to ssspeak truth to power.'

Policeman: 'Are you playing the fuckwit with me?'

Poet: 'No, because you'd be sssure to win.'

Policeman: 'Well, now, I think that warrants a little time in the cells! All right, boys, bang them up!'

Me: 'But . . . my brother is being awarded the Légion d'honneur!'

We were levitated into the wailing two-tone car.

I don't know why, but I immediately thought of a scene from *The Gendarme of St Tropez* (1964), where Louis de Funès and Michel Galabru run after a group of nudists on the beach to paint them blue. We used to watch it as a family every spring in Guéthary, in the living room that smelled of wood fires, floor polish and Johnnie Walker on the rocks. Another reference would be Pellos's comic strip *Les Pieds nickelés en plein suspense* (1963), but I couldn't work out which of us was Ribouldingue, and which was Filochard.

I had already been in the back of a police car once, during the Paris Salon du Livre in March 2004. I had tried to go up to President Chirac to give him a T-shirt emblazoned with the face of Gao Xingjian. The Chinese were the guests of honour at the Salon that year, but the winner of the 2000 Nobel Prize for Literature, a Chinese dissident living in exile in France and a naturalised Frenchman, had been bizarrely 'forgotten' by the organisers. Here, too, muscular arms had lifted me off the ground; here, too, I had found the experience somewhat mind-blowing. I have to admit, I was lucky that time: one of the guys carrying me got a reassuring message on his walkie-talkie.

'Don't beat him up, he's famous.'

That day, I thanked God for my notoriety. They released me after an hour, and the following day my brief incarceration made the front page of *Le Monde*. One hour spent banged up in a police van in order to seem like a fearless defender of human rights offered an excellent ratio of physical pain to media benefit. This time, they were going to lock me up for a little longer, for a cause that was significantly less philanthropic.

# 8

# THE ORIGINAL RAKE

Why Guéthary? Why does my only childhood memory constantly bring me back to the red and white mirage of the Basque Country, where the wind swells sheets pegged to washing lines like the sails of a motionless ship? I often think: *That's where I should have lived. I would be different; growing up there would have changed everything.* When I close my eyes, the sea at Guéthary dances beneath my eyelids, and it's as though I were opening the blue shutters of the old house. I gaze out of that window and tumble into the past; suddenly, I see us again.

A Siamese cat is scampering out of the garage door. We head down to the beach, me, my brother Charles and my aunt Delphine, who is the same age as us (she is my mother's youngest sister), with buttered ginger cake wrapped in tin foil, rolled-up beach towels under our arms. Along the way, my heart beats faster as we come to the train tracks, for fear of having an accident as my father did in 1947 when he was my age. He was carrying a kayak, one end of which was clipped by the San Sebastian train and he was dragged along the tracks, bleeding profusely, his hip ripped open along the metal rail, his skull fractured, his pelvis crushed. Ever since, there has been a sign at the crossing advising walkers: 'Warning, one train may hide another.' But my heart is also beating faster because I hope we might see the girls who man the level-crossing barrier. Isabelle and Michèle Mirailh had golden skin, green eyes, perfect teeth, denim dungarees cut off at the knee. My grandfather didn't approve of us hanging around with them, but it's not my fault if the world's most beautiful women are socially disadvantaged; that is surely God trying to re-establish some semblance of justice here on earth. It hardly mattered anyway, since they only had eyes for Charles, who looked straight through them. They would light up as he passed – 'Hey, there's the blond Parisian boy' – and Delphine would proudly say, 'So you remember my nephew?' He walked ahead of me down the hill towards the sea, a golden prince with indigo eyes, a boy so perfect in his polo shirt and white Lacoste Bermuda shorts walking towards the beach in slow motion, his polystyrene body-board sticking out under his arm, amid the burgeoning terraces of hydrangeas . . . then the smiles of the girls would fade as they saw me trotting along behind, a tousled skeleton with uncoordinated limbs, a sickly clown with incisors broken in a game of conkers in the Bagatelle gardens, knees crusted with purple scabs, a peeling nose, clutching the latest contraption to come free with *Pif Gadget*. It was not that they were repulsed by my appearance, but when Delphine introduced me, their eyes were elsewhere: 'And, er . . . this is Frédéric, his little brother.' I blushed to the tips of the jug ears that stuck out from my blond mop. I couldn't bring myself to speak, paralysed with shyness.

I spent my whole childhood struggling not to blush. If someone spoke to me, scarlet blotches appeared on my cheeks. If a girl looked at me, my cheekbones took on a garnet hue. If a teacher asked me a question in class, my face flushed purple. Out of necessity I had perfected techniques to hide my blushes: retying my shoelace, turning round as though there were something fascinating behind me, setting off at a run, hiding my face behind my hair, taking off my jumper.

The Mirailh sisters, sitting on the low whitewashed wall by the edge of the train track, swung their legs in the burst of sunshine between summer showers while I did up my laces, breathing in the damp earth. But they paid me no heed: I thought I was beet red, but in fact I was transparent. Thinking back about my invisibility still makes me angry, it filled me with such terrible sadness, such loneliness and bewilderment! I bit my nails, I had a terrible complex about my protruding chin, my elephant's ears and my skeletal thinness, which made me the butt of taunts at school. Life is a vale of tears, there's nothing to be done: never in my life did I have more love to give than I did on that day, but the girls who manned the barrier wanted none of it, and my brother was not to blame if he was better-looking than me. Isabelle showed him a bruise on her thigh: 'Look, yesterday I fell off my bike, see there? Here, touch it, *ow!* not too hard, you're hurting me . . .', while Michèle tried to charm Charles by leaning back, her long black hair streaming, her eyes closing like those dolls whose eyes shut when you lie them down and open again when you sit them up. Oh my fair damsels, if you but knew how little he cared about you! Charles was fretting about the game of Monopoly we would pick up again that night, about his mortgaged houses on the rue de la Paix and the avenue Foch; even at the age of nine he lived the life he does today, with the world at his feet, the universe bending to his conqueror's whims, and in that perfect life there was no place for you. I can understand your admiration (we always want what we cannot have), because I admired my triumphant elder brother as much as you did, I was so proud to be his younger brother I would have followed him to the ends of the earth – 'Oh brother who art dearer to me than the brightness of day' – and that's why I don't resent you; quite the opposite, I am grateful to you: if you had loved me from the first, would I ever have written?

This memory came back to me spontaneously: when you are in prison, childhood floats back to the surface. Perhaps what I took for amnesia was merely freedom.

# 9

# A FRENCH NOVEL

All four of my grandparents were dead before I was truly curious about their lives. Children take their own immortality for a generality, but their parents' parents pass away without giving them time to ask all their questions. By the time when, having become parents themselves, children finally want to know where they came from, the graves no longer answer.

Between the two world wars, love reasserted itself; couples came together; I am a distant result of those couples.

Sometime around 1929, the son of a doctor in Pau who had hacked off a number of legs at Verdun attended a recital at the Conservatoire Américain in Fontainebleau, where he was doing his military service. A widowed singer (born in Dalton, Georgia) by the name of Nellie Harben Knight was performing Schubert lieder, arias from *The Marriage of Figaro* and Puccini's famous '*O mio babbino caro*' wearing a long white dress trimmed with lace – at least I hope so. I found a photo of Nellie wearing that dress in an edition of the *New York Times* dated 23 October 1898, which states: 'Her voice is a clear, sympathetic soprano of extended range and agreeable quality.' My great-grandmother with her 'clear soprano' was accompanied on her tours by her daughter Grace, who well deserved her Christian name. A willowy blonde girl, with blue eyes permanently fixed on her piano keys, like the heroine of a Henry James novel, she was the daughter of a colonel in the British Army in India who died in 1921 of Spanish influenza: Morden Carthew-Yorstoun met and married Nellie in Bombay, having earlier served in the Zulu War in South Africa, with Lord Kitchener in the Sudan, and having led a New Zealand regiment, the Poona Horse, during the Boer War with Winston Churchill under his command. The soldier from Pau managed to catch the eye of this orphan of intriguing ancestry, and later to hold her hand during some frenzied waltzes, foxtrots and Charlestons. They discovered they shared the same sense of humour, the same love of Art – Jeanne Devaux, young Béarnais's mother, had been a painter (she had notably painted a portrait of Marie, wife of the poet Paul-Jean Toulet, in Guéthary), a profession almost as exotic as that of a singer. The young man from south-west France suddenly became an ardent music lover who regularly attended the soirées at the Conservatoire Américain. Charles Beigbeder and Grace Carthew-Yorstoun met up whenever he was on furlough; he lied about his age: born in 1902, at twenty-six he should have been long since married. But he loved poetry, music and champagne. The prestige conferred by his uniform (Grace, after all, was a soldier's daughter) did the rest. Young Grace never returned to New York. The couple were married at the town hall of the 16th arrondissement on 28 April 1931. They had two boys and two girls; the second son, born in 1938, was my father. On the death of his own father, young Charles inherited a spa in Pau: the 'Sanatorium of the Pyrenees'. It was a vast property of nearly two hundred acres (forests, copses, meadows, gardens) rising to a peak among the hills of Jurançon, at an altitude of 335 metres. As in *The Magic Mountain*, a well-to-do clientele in dinner jackets contemplated the spectacular sunsets over the central Pyrenees and, to the north, the expansive vista over the town of Pau and the Gave valley. It was hard to resist the call of the forests of mature pines and oaks, where children could gambol freely before being packed off to boarding school – in those days, parents did not raise their children themselves, and, as we will later see, that's still true to some extent. Charles Beigbeder resigned from his position as a solicitor with no regrets and took my grandmother to breathe the healing air of Béarn, where she could yell at the servants to her heart's content and forge bonds with the local British community. With money from his wife and his mother, my grandfather invested in my father's business. Soon our family owned a dozen sanatoriums in the region, renamed 'The Health Spas of Béarn', and my grandparents acquired the Villa Navarre, a superb house in Pau in the English cottage style, where Jean-Paul Toulet, Francis Jammes and Paul Valéry were regular visitors (family legend has it that the author of *Monsieur Teste* wrote his correspondence very early in the morning; the butler, whose name was Octave, used to grumble at having to wake at 4 a.m. to bring him his pot of coffee). A Catholic and a militant royalist, Charles Beigbeder looked like Paul Morand and was an assiduous reader of the far-right journal *Action française*, something which did not prevent him being elected president of the Cercle Anglais (exclusively male, it was, at the time, the most elegant club in Pau; he organised literary salons there). In the 1950s the family inherited a villa on the Basque coast, Cénitz Aldea (meaning 'Near Cénitz' in Basque) in Guéthary, a little village that had been fashionable since the Belle Époque. Tuberculosis did much for the fortunes of my family, and I have no hesitation in saying that the discovery of streptomycin by Selman Waksman around 1943 was an absolute catastrophe for my inheritance.

During the period we now call the interwar years (as though these young people could have anticipated that their post-war was also a pre-war), life was more austere in the great houses of the verdant Périgord. A countess who, as we know, had lost her husband in the second Battle of Champagne found herself alone at Quinsac, living in the château of Vaugoubert with two girls and two boys. In those days, Catholic war widows remained sexually faithful to their dead husbands. And of course, their children were called upon to sacrifice themselves. The two girls looked after their mother, something she encouraged in them – they did so for the rest of their lives. As for the two boys, they were automatically enrolled at the French military academy of Saint-Cyr, where an aristocratic 'de' in one's name was highly regarded. The elder boy agreed to marry an aristocratic girl who was not really his choice. Sadly, she quickly cuckolded him with a swimming instructor: the young man was heart-broken at being so poorly rewarded for his docility. He filed for divorce; in retaliation, his mother disinherited him. The younger brother, too, suffered misfortune: posted to the garrison at Limoges, he fell in love with a ravishing commoner, a dark-haired girl with blue eyes who danced atop pianos (problem number one), and whom he impregnated out of wedlock (problem number two). Their union had to rapidly be formalised: the marriage of Comte Pierre de Chasteigner de la Rocheposay and the ravishing Nicole Marcland, known as Nicky, took place on 31 August 1939, in Limoges. The date was ill-starred: the very next day, Germany invaded Poland. Bon Papa barely had time to invade Bonne Maman. The phoney war awaited him, in which the Maginot Line proved as unreliable as the rhythm method. Pierre found himself a prisoner. When he escaped, a nun having lent him civilian clothes and false papers, he returned to France to sire my mother. It was then that he learned that he too was to be disinherited, since his mother the countess found it difficult at Sunday Mass to acknowledge this marriage which was beneath her station, despite the fact that it had been celebrated by the local priest in the chapel of her own château. Curious are the customs of the Catholic aristocracy, which entail disinheriting those who are already more or less orphaned. The lineage of the Chasteigners de la Rocheposay goes back to the Crusades (I am descended from Hugues Capet, though I imagine that in this I am one of many), and includes a Bishop of Poitiers, who was ambassador in Rome to Henri II. Ronsard dedicated an ode to one of my ancestors, Anthoine, abbot of Nanteuil. Though written in 1550, these lines remained relevant to me on that fateful night's stay in January 2008:

*As time, so pass the trappings of this world*
*According to its motion*
*Life is fleet, and seasons, suddenly unfurl'd*
*Fast whither to a notion. [. . .]*
*Like a spring, young children grow*
*Then blossom in a summer*
*Surprised by winter they no longer show*
*What once they were.*

Despite the warning given to my great-great-grandfather by 'the Prince of Poets', my grandfather was thus sacrificed on the altar of the Great Passion.

In love, he made the same choice as the Duke of Windsor had three years earlier, and as Madame Cécilia Ciganer-Albeniz would sixty-eight years later when she married Nicolas Sarkozy: sacrificing château rather than happiness. When the war was over, Pierre de Chasteigner occupied Germany with his whole family for several years, in the Palatinate, then resigned his commission in 1949 so he would not be posted to Indochina. He was thus forced to investigate an activity no one in his lineage had attempted for about a millennium: work. He settled in a Paris apartment with shelves weighed down with volumes of the *Bottin Mondain* and the erotic works of Pierre Louÿs, on the rue de Sfax, while taking orders from his brother-in-law who ran a pharmaceutical laboratory. These were not his happiest years. When one no longer has the money to live like a king in Paris, one takes one's wife to the seaside to make a fourth in bridge and more children. Now, Nicky's father owned a house at Guéthary, of which she had fond memories. The Count and Countess decided to buy a little place there in return for a lifetime annuity to a Madame Damour, who had the good grace to shuffle off this mortal coil with little delay. So it was that the aristocratic military man and his six children moved in to Patrakénéa, directly opposite Cénitz

Aldea, the holiday resort of the bourgeois-bohemian, Americano-Béarnais, Beigbeder family. The reader should now begin to understand the strategic importance of this place. In Guéthary, my two families will become friends, and my father will shortly meet my mother.

# 10

## WITH FAMILY

I dreamed of being a free electron, but it is impossible to forever cut all ties with one's roots. To remember that child on the beach of Guéthary is to acknowledge that I come from somewhere, from a garden, from enchanted grounds, from a meadow that smells of new-mown grass and salt breezes, from a style of cooking redolent of stewed apple and stale bread.

I despise family score-settling, exhibitionistic autobiographies, psychoanalysis masquerading as literature and airing dirty laundry in public. François Mauriac, at the beginning of his *Mémoires intérieurs*, offers an object lesson in modesty: 'I will not speak of myself, so as not to oblige myself to speak of you.' Why do I not have the strength to remain silent? Is it possible to retain a little dignity when seeking to discover who one is and whence one came? I have a feeling that in my quest I will have to embroil many of those closest to me, both living or dead (I have already begun to do so). These people I love who did not ask to be rounded up in a book, as in some police raid. I suppose that every life has as many versions as it has narrators: we each have our own truth; let me make it clear from the outset that this account sets out only my own. In any case, it is not as though I am going to start bitching about my family at the age of forty-two. It so happens that I have no choice: I need to remember in order to grow old. A private detective investigating myself, I reconstruct my past from the scant clues at my disposal. I try not to cheat, but time has shuffled my memories, the way the pack of cards is shuffled before a game of Cluedo. My life is a whodunit in which the balm of memory embellishes by twisting each new piece of evidence.

In principle, every family has a history; but mine was short-lived: my family is composed of people who barely know each other. What is the purpose of a family? To grow apart. A family is the place of non-communication. My father has not spoken to his brother in twenty years. My mother's side of the family no longer sees my father's. As children, we see a lot of our family, mostly during holidays. Then parents split up, you see your father less frequently – *abracadabra*, half the family disappears. You grow up, holidays become less frequent, your mother's family grow more distant, until you only run into them at weddings, christenings and funerals – no one sends invitations to a divorce. When a nephew's birthday party or a Christmas dinner is organised, you find some excuse not to turn up: too much fear, the fear that they will see right through you, that you will be observed, criticised, confronted with your failings, recognised for what you are, weighed in the balance. The family brings back memories you had erased, rebukes you for your churlish amnesia. The family is a series of duties, a mob of people who knew you much too young, before you had grown up – and the oldest members are well placed to know that you have still not grown up. For a long time, I thought I could do without it. I was like Fitzgerald's boat in the last sentence of *The Great Gatsby*, beating 'against the current, borne back ceaselessly into the past'. In the end, I relived exactly what I had hoped to avoid. My two marriages foundered in indifference. I love my daughter more than anything, but I see her only on alternate weekends. The son of divorced parents, I divorced in turn, precisely because I had an allergy to 'family life'. Why does that phrase sound to me like a threat, even an oxymoron? It immediately conjures the image of a poor, harried man trying to install a child's car seat in an oval car. Needless to say, he hasn't had sex in months. Family life is a series of miserable meals where everyone rehashes the same humiliating anecdotes and hypocritical reflexes, where what you think of as family ties are nothing more than the lottery of birth and the rituals of communal living. A family is a group of people who cannot manage to communicate, and yet loudly interrupt each other, irritate each other, compare children's exam results and the décor of their homes, and scrabble over their parents' inheritance while the corpses are still warm. I don't understand how people can think of family as a place of safety, when in fact it triggers extreme panic. I always believed life began the moment one left one's family. Only then did we decide to be born. I considered life to be divided into two parts: the first was slavery, and one devoted the second part to attempting to forget the first. Being interested in one's childhood was for the dodderers and cowards. Having spent so long believing that it was possible to eliminate the past, I genuinely thought that I had managed to do so. Until today.

# 11

# END OF AN ERA

The last time I saw Pierre de Chasteigner, that majestic shrimp-fisher with his mane of white hair, was at the Curie Institute, in the 5th arrondissement, in 2004. My grandfather was laid out on a hospital bed, bald, gaunt, unshaven and delirious from the effects of the morphine. The public-alert sirens which go off at noon on the first Wednesday of every month began to wail. He talked to me about his time during the Second World War: 'Whenever you heard a siren, a bomb exploding, the roar of an aeroplane, it was good news: it meant you were still alive.'

An officer in the French army, Pierre de Chasteigner was wounded in the arm by shrapnel and captured near Amiens in 1940 during the phoney war. Narrowly avoiding the firing squad, he managed to escape using false papers.

'I should have joined the Resistance, but I was afraid; I thought it was better to go home.'

It was the first time he had raised the subject

with me. I suppose he saw his life flashing past; it was a pity he had to wait until he was dying to finally recover his memory. I didn't know what to say to him. He had lost as much weight as he had hair; his breathing was laboured. Tubes snaked in and out of his body, making alarming gurgling sounds.

'You have to understand, Frédéric, your uncle and your mother were already born. I had lost my father when I was two months old. It's hard, growing up without your papa.'

He knew that we had this weakness in common. I avoided the subject. Granny, too, had been an orphan – it's crazy when you think about it, my paternal grandmother and my maternal grandfather had both lost their soldier fathers. I come from a world with no fathers. My fisher of shrimp with his hollow cheeks went on: 'I didn't want to risk inflicting the same fate on my children, so I was a coward . . .'

The son of the man martyred on the battlefield at Champagne felt guilty that he had not been another martyr. I shook my head. 'Don't say things like that. You joined the Resistance, Bon Papa, you joined the O.R.A. in Limousin in 1943.'

'Yes, but I joined late, like Mitterrand.' (He pronounced it '*mitrand*'.) 'Frédéric, how could you ever have supported the communists?

Guingouin's men almost had me shot, you know. We were a competing organisation. They were very dangerous . . .'

I did not want to tell him I had supported the communists as an act of rebellion against my class, and therefore against him. I didn't dare say that I also saw communism as an extension of Christian charity by other means. Conversations between generations are rare; there is no time for digressions; lose the thread and you may never find it again (which is, in fact, what happened). The important thing was that my grandfather had never known his own father, because he was dead. My case was almost worse: I was deprived of a father who was still very much alive. My daughter probably suffers the same strange absence; the silence of the living is harder to understand than the silence of the dead. I should have taken my grandfather's hand, but we do not do physical affection in my family.

'Bon Papa, you were heroic to stay with your children; tough luck for France.'

As I said this, I knew I was asking for a slap in the face, but my grandfather was tired; he simply sighed. Afterwards he asked whether I prayed for him, and I lied. I said I did. He pressed the morphine pump; he was completely spaced out now: it's quite funny to think that our health system peddles class-A drugs to cancer patients quite legally, while those of us who get off our face in the street wind up in the nick (are we really any less ill?). By the time I left the clinic it was dark, as though someone had switched off the lights.

On his deathbed, my grandfather had more or less told me, 'Make love, not war.' At the last moment, the old commandant awarded the Military Cross '39–'45 became, ideologically, a *soixante-huitard*. It took me years before I understood what he was actually trying to tell me in that fatal moment: you don't remember the war, Frédéric, you weren't even born then, but your parents and grandparents still remember, even if subconsciously, and all your problems, and theirs, are directly linked to their suffering, their fear, to the bitterness and the hatred of that period in the history of France. Your great-grandfather was a hero of the First World War, your grandfather a veteran of the Second; do you really imagine such violence could not have consequences for successive generations? It is thanks to our sacrifice that you grew up in a country at peace, my dear grandson. Never forget what we went through, never forget your country. Never forget where you come from. Never forget me.

* * *

We buried him the following week, in the graveyard by the sea, in front of the Guéthary church, amid the stooping crosses, under the stone where my grandmother already waited, with a view of the ocean behind the hills; the green dingles married to the deep blue of the sea. During the ceremony, my cousin Margot Crespon, a hypersensitive young actress, read a quatrain or two by Toulet (an opium-eating poet who lies in the same graveyard as my morphine-swigging grandfather):

*Sleep, friend; tomorrow, higher*
*Wings your soul and steep.*
*Sleep as the gyrfalcon sleeps,*
*Or the covered fire.*

*While beneath the russet sun*
*The mayflies flitter,*
*Sleep beneath leaves so bitter.*
*My youth, too, is run.*

I chose this poem because it sounds like a prayer. Leaving the graveyard, I watched the sun dissolve among the branches of a cypress like a nugget of gold in a giant's hand.

# 12

# BEFORE THEY WERE MY PARENTS, THEY WERE NEIGHBOURS

In France, this was the post-war period, the Liberation, *les trente glorieuses* – the thirty glorious years of prosperity that followed – in short, the duty to forget that preceded our duty to remember. Guéthary was no longer as exclusive as it had been before the state mandated paid annual leave: 'holidaymakers' thronged the beaches every summer, jammed the roads, fouled the sand with greasy paper. On either side of the Chemin Damour my grandparents – maternal and paternal – railed against the democratisation of France. From the upper floor of the Beigbeder villa, Jean-Michel, wearing a white jumper, and leaning out over the balcony, could spy on what was taking place in the garden of the house opposite: the two Chasteigner girls, Christine and Isabelle, playing badminton, drinking orangeade, or getting dolled up to go to the *toro de fuego* on 14 July. I checked:

from the balcony of Cénitz Aldea there is still a view that plunges into the grounds of Patrakénéa, as into a young girl's cleavage. I too long to spy on the new neighbours whenever I go to take tea with my aunt Marie-Sol, who still lives in the Beigbeder villa (the Chasteigners' house was sold last year). This geographical topography plays a not insignificant role in the story of my life. Had my father not watched the Chasteigner girls across the road, I wouldn't be here to write about it. In my eyes, this blue-painted balcony is as hallowed as Shakespeare's balcony in Verona.

Seaside resorts are not all equal. Every beach along the Basque coast has its own unique personality. The large beach at Biarritz is our Cannes Croisette, with the Hôtel du Palais standing in for the pink-fronted Carlton, and the casino acting as a dilapidated Palm Beach Hotel. It's even possible to imagine you are on the seafront in Deauville, as you sit on a terrace ordering oysters and white wine, watching strolling families in shorts who have never heard of the Marquis de Cuevas's balls. The beach at Bidart is more family-friendly, it's the same bourgeois crowd with jumpers tied round their shoulders you find at Ars-en-Ré. It's best avoided unless you enjoy the screams of drowning children,

Hermès towels and hyphenated Christian names. Nicknamed 'the bastard of the Basques', the beach at Guéthary is wilder, more plebeian; it has a regional atmosphere and attracts a lot of former addicts in detox. It smells of deep-fried food and bargain-basement sun-cream; a small, crowded stretch of beach where bathers change in red-and-white-striped huts rented for the season. Even the waves differ from one beach to the next: vertical at Biarritz, dangerous at Bidart, higher at Guéthary. At Biarritz, the waves smash you onto the sand, at Bidart the riptide pulls you out to sea, at Guéthary the rollers crush you on the rocks. At Saint-Jean-de-Luz the sea wall has neutered the swell, which is why the old-age pensioners sitting on the benches talk of nothing but the wheeling seagulls and emergency rescue helicopters. The biggest waves are at Hendaye, including the legendary 'Belharra', a wave that rises to between fifteen and eighteen metres, tackled only by the most psychopathic surfers, who are pulled out to sea by jet skis. The beach at Alcyons is almost like a strand in Brittany, offering sea spray instead of atomisers, and shingle as a 'foot massage'; the Chambre d'Amour is a refuge for separatist romantics and pick-up artists nostalgic for the famous Rolls-Royce of champion windsurfer Arnaud de Rosnay; the Basque coast serves as a meeting point for drivers of VW microbuses that reek of whacky baccy and damp bikinis hung out to dry; La Madrague is snobbish, taking after Saint-Tropez, as its nickname suggests. The locals' favourite beach is called Erretegia, a splendid natural amphitheatre between Ilbarritz and Bidart. Its chief virtue is that Parisians don't know about it. Why do I only have memories of Cénitz? Is it simply because the Beigbeder villa at Guéthary was called Cénitz Aldea? Cénitz is morose, with sharp, jagged rocks and stinging sands. Cénitz is wild, disagreeable, depressing, gloomy. The waves that rise up there are big, heavy, frenzied, dirty, deafening. It is often very cold there. In the Basque Country, sunshine is a scarce commodity: you wait for it, at Sunday Mass the priest prays for its arrival, people talk about it endlessly, the moment it appears you rush to the Cent Marches or to La Plancha, and the following day it is raining as usual, but you don't give a damn because you don't wake up until 5 p.m. The sun may be unexpected at Guéthary, but how could anyone grow weary of such skies? The sky is a suspended ocean. From time to time it melts, washing the hillsides and the houses with seawater. My one memory of childhood unfolds on the least welcoming beach in France. My mind has not picked this spot at random. It was while heading down to Cénitz beach that my father nearly died at the age of nine, dragged along by a train. It was on the road to Cénitz that he met my mother, who was holidaying in the villa opposite. It was in this village that they married. Cénitz is a distillation of my whole life. In remembering this one place, I am encapsulating myself, condensing myself. To remember who one is at heart absolves one of having to remember the rest; my memory is lazy, it has preserved Cénitz like a crib-sheet, a mnemonic from which my whole life flows. Just like David Lynch's *Mulholland Drive*, the greatest of all films about amnesia, where a simple blue key is enough to reconstruct a shattered life. Imagine a buzzing noise in the background, steadily growing louder, making the scene more dramatic as we come to the thermonuclear core of my story. I am going to draw you a map so you can see it more clearly.

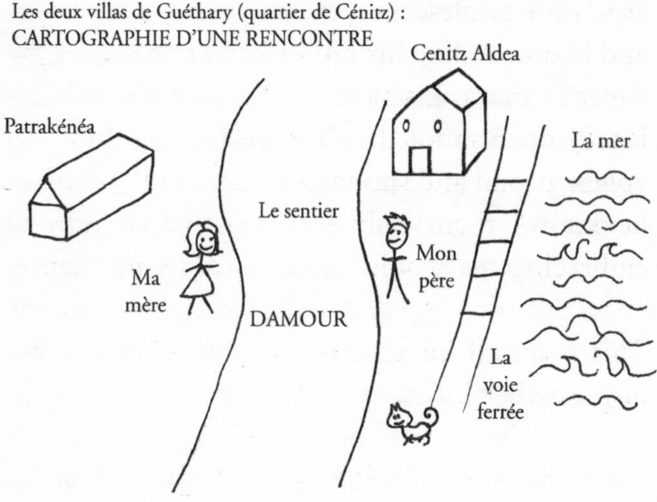


Maman: very young, with fine blonde hair, wearing a light dress, pale azure eyes, white teeth, shy and refined, a posh girl with impeccable manners, living proof that intelligence can rhyme with innocence, eager to escape her starchy aristocratic family, hopelessly romantic, sublime in both body and soul. Ready for a long life of poetry, of love, of pleasure, she will offer herself to . . .

Papa: a young, slim, rich man, somewhat overshadowed by his elder brother, he is studious, and at the age of eighteen he travelled round the world. He is focused and passionate, he has piercing green eyes, he is funny without being cruel, an adolescent curious about philosophy and literature like his father, keen to conquer the America that is his mother, relaxed without being blasé, open-minded, pleasure-seeking but not vulgar, proud and smiling, he hates snobs because he knows them only too well, he dreams of embracing the whole world, and my mother.

This is how I imagine them, from photographs, in the twin glories of their youth.

My father steps out of Cénitz Aldea wearing an alpaca suit, a copy of Plotinus' *Enneads* tucked under one arm.

My mother steps out of Patrakénéa in a polka-dot dress, carrying a seven-inch single by the Platters.

The road between them is called the *Sentier Damour* – the Path of Love – you couldn't make it up.

I am trying to imagine this meeting, without which I would not now be sitting in this cell, clasping my knees. My mother is sixteen, my father nineteen. 'Her little sister had the bigger breasts, but I chose the elder; I chose, who knows why,' my father confided to me forty years later in the Extreme-Orient restaurant. He is being unduly modest: I know he was crazy about her, and she about him. One evening, my father slips his arm around my mother's waist during the *toro del fuego*. Later, in the back of my father's 2CV, they embrace, and it is wonderful, the universe is flawless; in those moments everything seems obvious – but why do I say 'those moments', plural, when we all know such a moment is unique – I too have only felt it once. They both instantly fell head over heels, something that never happens, please let me believe that it did, it's a thought that comforts me.

Several summers later, they shyly notice each other, they go to the beach together or to Mass, drink lemonade (my father can't abide alcohol), maybe go to a dance, they ride their bikes, complain about their families, stare out to sea, and probably build castles in the air. They meet up again in Paris after their first kiss, in secret, on the rue des Sablons, in the young man's bachelor pad. It is here that they knew each other Biblically, long before they were married. Please don't hold this lack of professionalism against me, but I'd rather not imagine the details of my parents' sex life. I picture a moment both beautiful and awkward, tender and fearful, wonderful and terrifying. For a long time my mother was afraid of getting pregnant while still a minor: in those days, the age of majority was twenty-one.

There were lots of parties on the Basque coast in those days. People would go to the villa of Denise Armstrong, a model and couturier who was friends with Josephine Baker (pronounced 'Back-air'), in Bayonne, where they might meet the Villalongas, the Duke of Tamames – nicknamed 'Kiki' – the Horn y Prados, Guy d'Arcangues or André-Pierre Tarbès. Every Wednesday, young people would meet up at the Casino Bellevue, at Sonny's in Biarritz or at the Éléphant Blanc . . . You could read accounts of these wild nights in the local paper, under the by-line of 'Baroness Bigoudi' – 'the Baroness in Curlers'. Marisa Berenson came to take tea at Cénitz Aldea, during the period when she was stepping out with Arnaud de Rosnay. Peter Viertel, the husband of Deborah Kerr and screenwriter of *The African Queen*, had discovered the Basque coast while shooting Hemingway's *The Sun Also Rises*, and imported the Californian longboard to Biarritz's beaches. This very 'with-it' couple welcomed visitors to their home in Saint-Jean-de-Luz. My father hated society life, but his elder sister hung out with all the celebrities trailing my future parents in her perfumed wake. It both impressed and irritated my mother-to-be.

Hand in hand, Marie-Christine and Jean-Michel took off for the United States in order to finish their studies (my father at Harvard, my mother at Mount Holyoke), but above all to be together, far from their strict parents, their moribund country, far from the folly of the post-war period.

And then they came back. Above the village of Guéthary stands the old church where they married on 6 July 1963: he is wearing a top hat and a fitted grey morning coat (thirty years later, when I wore the same thing in the church of Baux-de-Provence, I looked just as grotesque), my mother wears a white dress and flowers in her blonde hair. At my parents' house in Neuilly I saw Super-8 footage of the ceremony when I was little, projected onto a rolled-down screen in the living room. Granny had drawn the blinds, and I don't think I have ever seen anything more ravishing. It is the only time in my life that I caught Jean-Michel Beigbeder unawares placing a kiss on the lips of Countess Marie-Christine de Chasteigner de la Rocheposay d'Hust et du Saint Empire, 'And other places visible only at low tide,' added my father during the screening, and in the background the clacking of the cogs that operated the projector sounded like a metronome set to maximum speed. My mother had her hair teased into a beehive, like Brigitte Bardot in *Le Mépris* – the film came out the same year; my father is thin, his head drawn into his starched shirt-collar; they are surrounded by Basque dancers; to the sound of the drums and the flutes the young newlyweds bow their heads and pass under an archway of flowers, a choir of singers dressed in red and white form a guard of honour. I remember all this because I found it impossible to believe that this young couple, barely more than teenagers, obviously in love, shy, surrounded by countless family members, could be my parents. Sadly, this piece of evidence was lost during the many subsequent house moves by its two leading actors. Later, my mind managed to forget them as a couple. I never knew them together; my only memories of them are from after their separation – as though I had tossed them into my mental trashcan, before clicking 'empty recycle bin' on my internal hard drive.

My big brother was born the following year. Then I foolishly chose 1965 to make my entrance into this world: it was a little early, I shouldn't have been in such a hurry to be born. We were both wanted, yet unexpected, babies. We arrived too quickly, too close together; that was not how my parents had planned things, they were forced to reorganise. My father insisted on naming my elder brother after his father (Charles), my mother christened me Frédéric after the hero of Flaubert's *Sentimental Education*, who is a failure. My parents split up soon afterwards. Have you noticed that fairy tales all end on the wedding day? I, in my turn, married twice, and each time I experienced the same fear, that stopped me in my tracks at the moment of saying 'I do', that disagreeable suspicion that the best was already behind us.

# 13

# REVELATIONS ABOUT THE LAMBERTS

Évelyne and Marie-Sol Beigbeder, my father's elder sisters, told me about something that took place at the Villa Navarre during the last war. This story not only allows me to boast about the virtues of my paternal grandparents, but it also shows why it is sometimes necessary to break the law. The law is not always right – especially in France. For example, in 1940, the French law passed by the Vichy government led by Pierre Laval decreed that Pau was in the *Zone Libre*, whereas in Paris the wearing of the yellow star was obligatory for a certain sector of the population. As we know, Pierre de Chasteigner later regretted that he did not join the Resistance earlier – but he did so nonetheless. As to the town of Pau, it quintupled in size, the exodus from the occupied zone having brought a large number of Jews persecuted in their own country by the French police. And so, in June 1940, a network of Christian friends secretly suggested to Charles and Grace Beigbeder that they hide a Jewish family who had been forced to flee Paris leaving all their belongings. The discussions around the large dining table were convoluted. I would have loved to have been a fly on the wall . . .

Charles: 'As long-time supporters of *Action Française*, should we refuse to welcome these Jews under our roof? I spoke to Maurras, at Saint-Rémy de Provence. He was so deaf I had to shout in his ear in front of everyone that we are anti-German. He replied, "Ah! Your wife is English, you will be forgiven much!"'

Grace: 'We are Catholics first and foremost, and the Archbishop of Toulouse did say that "The Jews are men, the Jews are women [ . . .] they form part of the human race, they are our brothers." No Christian should forget that.'

Charles: 'Darling, you know that these people will attract the attention of the police and the Germans. Do I have to remind you that your native land is not exactly on the same side as the Boche? We risk being deported if they find out we are hiding Jews. Are you sure you want to endanger our own children to save the "Lamberts" [what a ridiculous name to choose, you can tell it's fake a mile away], people we don't even know?'

Grace: 'Octave, have the rooms on the second floor made up for them, four or five people can easily hide out there without anyone being any the wiser. Listen, these are friends of friends, we have no choice.'

Charles: 'I agree. But we need to lay down some rules: they are to eat upstairs, one meal a day, no going out, no walking in the park, no contact with the children, officially they are lodgers who live upstairs, that's all.'

Grace: 'God save the King and the British Navy!'

There were four of them: the grandmother, the father who was a jeweller, a little boy named Michel and a maid. The living arrangements went as well as could be expected, that is to say they were marked by a mutual caution. The Beigbeder children were not allowed to go up to the second floor; their parents told them nothing about these unobtrusive lodgers. The Lamberts led a clandestine, reclusive life, a self-imposed and agonising imprisonment. The three cows from the farm at the bottom of the garden supplied ten litres of milk a day. One particular day has remained famous in the family annals, the day a German officer visited the Villa Navarre. According to my aunts, it would have been in September 1943. The Obersturmführer admired the view of the Pyrenees, the beautiful French-style garden, the opulence of the house. He rang the front doorbell and Grace, my American grandmother, had the presence of mind to call all her children (Gérald and Marie-Sol, Évelyne and my father) and tell them to run around making lots of noise, to dash up and down the stairs, play tag in the living room and the library like horrid, badly brought-up brats.

The smell in the hall is the smell of my father's childhood: a mixture of floor polish, of the linoleum in the lifts, of dried flowers and must . . . It still lingers in the lobby of the villa, which is now a luxury hotel. Despite the renovations that converted our basement playroom into an indoor swimming pool, the smell of the past does not fade; I constantly find myself wishing someone would open the windows and smell the Pyrenees. The officer climbed the front steps in 1943, breathing the same odour as you would were you to book a room for the night. The caretaker, Catherine, and her husband Léon ran to warn the 'Lamberts' on the second floor; the sequestered family's pulse rates must have shot up on seeing, through the fanlights, the vehicles of the Reichswehr parked in the large driveway. The

German officer was very proper: no Nazi salute, merely a kiss on Madame Beigbeder's hand as he clicked his heels.

'What a lovely house you have, Madame! Might it be possible to visit, *bitte schön*? We are looking for a place in which to billet ourselves.

Granny coughed: 'It's just that . . . as you can see, we are a large family, and all the rooms are occupied, sadly.' (Another coughing fit.) 'The house is full, what with the children, the servants, the chauffeur, the chambermaids, the cook . . . And besides, we would not want to put you in danger. We are looking after a number of contagious patients.'

'My dear Madame, you do realise that I can requisition this house under the exigencies of war.'

'But of course, if you really wish to, a few minuscule germs will hardly upset the Wehrmacht, will they?'

At this juncture, my grandfather's mother came down the stairs, asking: 'What's going on here, Grace? Who is this man?'

'Don't worry, Madame, we are just chatting with this courteous officer.'

'Who is this old woman?' asked the German officer, in French.

'Oh, allow me to introduce my mother-in-law,

the famous painter Jeanne Devaux; she lives with us. And if you'll forgive me, Lieutenant, in French one does not say "old woman", one says "elderly lady".'

Then the cows trooped across the courtyard. The officer stared, astonished. 'What is that?'

'There is a farm next door . . .'

'What about the second floor? Have you no room for us there?'

An agonising silence. At that point Jeanne displayed great presence of mind. 'Ah no,' she said. 'On the second floor, we keep the hay for the cows!'

'*Ach so!* Thank you for your warm welcome, we will think over your invitation and will come back, perhaps. *Auf wiedersehen!*'

The officer never returned.

The Lamberts left the Villa Navarre after the German army retreated in August 1944. As she climbed into her car, the grandmother, Simone, declared, 'Four bloody years wasted! I can't wait to get back to Paris!' This thankless outburst apparently shocked my parents. They never spoke of the episode again, nor did they keep in touch with the family of diamond merchants. Is it possible to save Jews while remaining loyal to a Catholicism that is royalist, traditional and vaguely anti-Semitic? Snobs are routinely accused of being superficial, but let us not forget that they can be thoughtlessly heroic, can save an entire family merely because they are of the same social class. Though in doing so my family took great pains to keep their distance, as though exclaiming, 'Just because we've saved your lives doesn't give you the right to take liberties!'

Meanwhile, my grandmother's retort, 'One does not say "old woman", one says "elderly lady",' went all round Pau at the time, like many one-liners from Granny, who was distantly related to George Bernard Shaw, and whose own father, a colonel in the Indian army, used to say, 'I managed to tame India but I've never been able to tame my daughter.'

My favourite saying of Granny's is one that François Bayrou related to me: during a cocktail party at the Villa Navarre for the opening of the fox-hunting season, when he politely asked her how she was, she replied, 'It's dreadful! The older I get, the more intelligent I get.' My aunt Évelyne also told me that Charles and Grace Beigbeder employed a number of Jewish doctors (German, Hungarian, Polish) at the Pic du Midi sanatorium for the duration of the war, listing them as 'interns', and they also hid a number of Jewish children, whom they passed off as tuberculosis patients. The Germans had a great fear of germs; they never went near the sanatoriums. The Princesse de Faucigny-Lucinge, *née* Ephrussi, having arrived in Pau from the avenue Foch with a retinue of twenty staff, chose to spend a night at the Villa Navarre, fearful of being disturbed by some unexpected visit. My cousin Anne Lafontan estimates that some five hundred Jews passed through the family's health spas to escape into Spain. Sadly, there is no proof of these heroic acts, something that makes my father's grandparents unsung heroes of extraordinary courage. I know that Grace smoked English cigarettes given to her by a friend, Father Carré, who sheltered British pilots, all of them aristocrats, and that her favourite sport was to blow British smoke in the faces of the German soldiers strolling along the boulevard des Pyrénées. Charles was twice arrested during train trips to Paris. He only managed to get home thanks to friends in high places, but who were they? My uncle maintains that he also saved collaborators during the *Épuration légale*, the purge that followed the liberation of France, who escaped to Spain following the same route that had saved so many Jews. It does not amount to much, but it's all I know: my family played an extraordinary double role (both supporters of Pétain and supporters of de Gaulle were welcomed at the Villa Navarre, but were made to use different entrances so they did not bump into each other). Now that the house has been turned into a Relais et Château, it is possible for anyone to sleep in Granny's bedroom, which my grandfather kept pristine and unchanged for years after her death. I remember it as a hallowed sanctuary which I was forbidden to enter. I went back there after the house had been turned into a hotel. They say it is a mistake to revisit childhood haunts, because they seem smaller. Not so the Villa Navarre: it is the only house that does not shrink with time. After the conversion, any budding writer could sleep in this dead woman's bedroom. But Granny still haunts it, and this particular occupant will swear that, on certain nights, he heard her voice whispering in that New York drawl: 'One does not say "this dead woman's bedroom", Frédéric, one says "the apartments of my late lamented grandmother".'

My country was Nazi while my parents were children. Disgusted by France, my father and mother went off to study in America, the country that had liberated theirs. My mortified grandparents managed to save face thanks to a general exiled in London. Until May 1968, when hypocrisy was dashed to pieces, and with it my parents' marriage. It was only in May 1981, with the election of an ex-member of the Resistance from Vichy as president, that it became possible for my grandparents to recognise that they were survivors: on my mother's side, a wounded soldier, prisoner of war and patriarch, a man who had come late to the Resistance but one who had actually fought; on my father's side, a monarchist imbued with the anti-Semitic ideas of Charles Maurras, prosperous during the Occupation, and yet 'Righteous Among the Nations', though never acknowledged as such by Israel since no one ever asked. It is probable that it would do Charles Beigbeder Senior a fat lot of good to have a tree planted in his name at Yad Vashem; yet this completely forgotten episode in my grandfather's life, which I never would have known about had I not dragged it out of my uncles and aunts, fills me with pride, me the idiot younger son currently squatting in a police cell. As the Talmud says, 'Whoever saves one life, saves the world entire.' After the First World War, the devastated French understood that it was better to be cunning and alive than heroic and dead. And when they were heroes, it was at inopportune moments; they did not boast about it, sometimes it happened almost by accident. One could be a hero and a diplomat, heroic and a socialite, heroic despite being rich, heroic without dying. People considered themselves lucky to be alive in a country that had given up the ghost.

# 14

# HEARING PROBLEMS

The cops are nice enough, but service is slow: it takes them a ridiculous amount of time to bring me a couple of plastic cups filled with tap water. I waste my energy constantly peering through the glass and asking the time. Finally a uniformed policewoman answers: 7 a.m. Panic cranks up a notch when you have a hangover. It's impossible to sleep with the screams and sobs of the others doing 'cold turkey'. You come down to earth with a bump. Sarij 8 is a temporary prefab hut. Even so, it has a very chic address: 210, rue du Faubourg Saint-Honoré, a short stroll from the Élysée Palace on the other side of the road. Sarij looks like a lean-to shanty bolted to the town hall of the 8th arrondissement like scaffolding. This is where they buried me, after strip-searching and photographing me, in this plywood caravan. My head is exploding, I have an urge to throw up, suffocating behind the shatterproof Securit glass. The Turkish toilet is a stinking hole at the far end of a corridor lit by fluorescent tubes. Prisoners are forbidden to close the door. Breakfast is served: a limp biscuit and a carton of warm orange juice. Aversion to the metallic clang of the three bolts being shot home as the police officer locks the cell when you come back from the toilet, or when he brings you the cup of lukewarm water you've been begging for for three-quarters of an hour. At that point you keep a grip on yourself so as not to stick your foot in the door, or pound on it, begging to be let out. What did Beau Brummell do to maintain his dignity when he was imprisoned in Caen in 1835? After an infinite length of time, a plain-clothes policeman tells me he's going to interview me in his office. We go up to the third floor, into a room whose walls are covered with photos of missing persons. In the United States they put them on milk cartons; it's certainly a lot more useful than plastering them in an office where no one will see them except drunken revellers and juvenile delinquents. Taking off his battered leather jacket, the officer asks what got into us, the Poet and me, to commit a flagrantly illegal act on the public highway. He is wearing a black polo shirt buttoned to the throat; you get the feeling he's trying to look like David Caruso in a re-run of *NYPD Blue*. He recognises me, and seems happy to be sharing a scene in his TV series with another star of the small screen. I explain that our actions were a homage to the chapter in Bret Easton Ellis's *Lunar Park* where Jay McInerney snorts coke off the bonnet of a Porsche in Manhattan (Jay insists Bret made it up, but I don't believe it). The cop has never heard of them, so I explain that these two American novelists have had a significant influence on my work. I invoke my solidarity with cigarette-smokers, henceforth compelled by law to indulge their vice in the street. I tell him about my fascination with the Prohibition era in the States in the Twenties, and how it inspired the alcoholic Fitzgerald to create the character of Gatsby the bootlegger. To my great surprise, the cop quotes Jean Giono at me: 'Did you know he got the idea for *The Horseman on the Roof* while he was in prison during the Liberation?' I must be imagining things. I quote him the only sentence of Giono I can remember: 'My book is finished, all that remains is for me to write it.' It sums up my current situation pretty well. The cop is extolling the virtues of incarceration on creative-writing. I thank him for the cramped conditions of my cell, which are indeed expanding my imaginative horizons.

'Thank you, officer, for enrolling me in the Dread Poets Society: François Villon, Clément

Marot, Miguel de Cervantes, Casanova in *I Piombi*, Voltaire and Sade in the Bastille, Paul Verlaine at Mons, Oscar Wilde in Reading Gaol, Dostoevsky in the penal colony at Omsk . . . [I could have added Jean Genet in Frènes, Céline in Denmark, Albertine Sarrazin, Alphonse Boudard, Édouard Limonov, Nan Aurousseau . . .] Thank you, Inspector, all I need to do now is to write my "From the House of the Undead", my 'Ballad of Champs-Élysées Gaol"!'

He types out my statement on an old computer; I see he's not as technologically well equipped as Jack Bauer. He asks, 'Why do you take drugs?'

'That's a pretty big word.'

'Why do you consume this toxic product?'

'The quest for fleeting pleasures.'

Now you know that, somewhere in the archives of the national police force, there exists a deposition in which one Frédéric Beigbeder declared that the use of narcotics was a 'quest for fleeting pleasures'. Your taxes have been put to good use. When Jean-Claude Lamy asked her the same question a few years earlier, Françoise Sagan replied, 'One takes drugs because life is deathly dull, because people are tiresome, because there are so few great ideas still worth defending, because one lacks drive.'

'Do you want to die?'

'Listen, Commissioner, my health is none of your business, as long as it doesn't affect your own.'

'Are you self-destructive?'

'No, I'm bored. And that shouldn't be your problem!'

He asks me to elaborate, and I outline my opposition to a society that claims to protect people from themselves, to stop them from recreational self-harming, as though there is any other way for a human being to live than by accumulating pleasant vices and deadly addictions. He answers that he did not make the laws, but is simply enforcing them . . . A hackneyed refrain. I restrain myself from telling him how my family disobeyed the anti-Semitic laws during the war. I simply bow my head, and sigh; the French judicial system has one thing in common with the Catholic faith: it encourages the *mea culpa*. I feel as though I am the little boy I once was, summoned to the abbot's office at the Lycée Bossuet for some idiocy or other. The inspector continues: 'But you're not just hurting yourself. You have a daughter.'

'A neurotic disposition. I have noticed I have a tendency to push those I love away. If you've got a couch, I can explain why. Do you have three years to spare?'

'No, but I have twenty-four hours, or forty-eight, maybe even seventy-two. I can extend your time in custody as long as necessary. You are a public figure, you are setting a bad example. We can allow ourselves to be a little harsher with you than with anyone else.'

'According to Michel Foucault, the idea of "biopolitics" was born in the eighteenth century, when the state began to quarantine lepers and plague victims. And yet France is the country of human rights. Which authorises me to claim the Right to Singe My Wings, the Right to Fall From a Great Height, the Right to Sink to the Depths. These are the Human Rights that ought to feature in the Preamble to the Constitution, along with the Right to Cheat on Your Wife Without Being Photographed in the Newspapers, the Right to Sleep with a Prostitute, the Right to Smoke a Cigarette on a Plane or to Drink Whisky on a Television Set, the Right to Make Love without a Condom with Persons who Accept the Risks, the Right to Die with Dignity when Afflicted with an Excruciating Terminal Illness, the Right to Snack Between Meals, the Right Not to Eat Your Five-a-Day, the Right to Sleep with a Consenting Sixteen-Year-Old Without Her Filing a Complaint Five Years Later for Corruption of a Minor . . . would you like me to go on?'

'We're getting off the subject. Drugs are a scourge that destroys the lives of hundreds of thousands of young people who didn't have the same opportunities as you. You're from a good family, I can tell you earn a good living, you went to university. You've got nothing to complain about.'

'Oh no! Not you, not that! Because I'm middle-class I have no right to complain? I've had that shit trotted out to me all my life!'

'Most of the criminals locked up here are very poor. It's easier to understand why they go off the rails . . .'

'If the rich were all happy, capitalism would always be right, and your job would be a lot less interesting.'

'You don't understand the damage this shit does. I see it every day. Cocaine has flooded every *département*, the towns, the suburbs, even the villages; teenagers deal it in playgrounds! What will you say when your daughter is offered drugs at school?'

Now there he got me; the question stopped me dead. I thought long and hard before answering. It was the first and probably the last time that I would have a socio-philosophical discussion with a cop who'd just banged me up. I wanted to make the most of it.

'If at the age of forty-two I flout the law, it's because I didn't disobey my mother enough when

I was young. I have twenty years of disobedience to make up for. I warn my daughter about the dangers that threaten her. But I would never be angry with a child for being disobedient: that is how children assert themselves. Of course I scold my daughter when she throws a tantrum, but I would be a lot more worried if she never did. I am going to write a book about my childhood. Since you are treating me like a kid, I am going to try to become one again. So I can explain to my daughter that pleasure is a very serious thing: necessary, but dangerous. Don't you realise that this business goes beyond both of us? What's at stake here is our way of life. Instead of knocking the victims, ask yourself why so many young people feel hopeless, why they're bored to death, why they seek out any extreme sensation to avoid the grim destiny of the frustrated consumer, the normalised individual, the pre-formatted, pre-programmed jobless zombies.'

'I'm a cop, you're a writer. We each have our job. Now, when some kid sets fire to a car, we catch him, we question him and we send him to court. You on the other hand, you try to work out the reasons for this nihilistic revolt . . . I'll leave that to you.'

'What you refuse to understand is that this drug is just a pretext for feeling closer to others, a means of expression between strangers, a way of staving off loneliness, a stupid but a very real connection between lost souls . . . If you know something else that's as effective at facilitating social interaction between misfits, please, tell me.'

'OK, OK . . . But I can't help wondering how you'll manage to write about your childhood.'

'Really? And why's that exactly?'

'Well, everyone knows . . .'

'Everyone knows what?'

'Come on, everyone knows coke makes you lose your memory.'

He was more than a match for me, this cop. I was floored. He had just made me realise why I'd been struggling in my dungeon to remember all the things I'd forgotten. The job of a cop is like the job of a novelist; it consists of linking seemingly unconnected things. We had something in common, he and I: the conviction that there is no such thing as chance. I digested this information, then gathered my wits: 'You're right, coke does make you lose your memory. You live intensely in the present, and feel like shit the day after. It's the drug of choice for people who don't want to remember, don't want to hope. Coke burns up your legacy; I'm writing about it because it's a symbol of our times. I write about cocaine in my books not to be "down with the kids" or "street" (if that's what I wanted, I'd need to write about something less old-school: ketamine, MDMA, GBH, 2CB, DMT, PCP, BZP . . .), but because it sums up our era: it's a metaphor for a perpetual present, with no past, no future. Believe me, a drug like this couldn't help but dominate the world today; we are only at the beginning of a planetary intoxication.'

'I hope you're wrong . . .'

'So do I.'

I feel my words ring false; even I am not swallowing my spiel, I feel ridiculous defending some drugged-up rebellious persona at 8 a.m., in an office that smells of cold coffee and sweaty armpits. Who do I think I am, my alter-ego Octave? The cop held out the copy of my statement he had just printed off.

'Read it through and sign at the bottom. The interview is over. I'm going to take you back to your cell and fax my report to the public prosecutor.'

'When will I get out?'

'The quicker I send the fax, the sooner the magistrate will decide if and when to let you go. But don't bank on it being before eleven: he doesn't get into the office before then . . . And since you're "a celeb", he'll insist on taking charge of your case personally.'

'But can't you do anything? I'm claustrophobic, I'm going crazy in there, it's horrible . . .'

'I know: that's the general idea. Police custody cells are deliberately designed to unsettle you, make you more likely to confess everything. But don't worry, your case is pretty routine. You should be out by noon.'

That turned out not to be true, though he didn't know it. The inspector took me back to my cage, smiling. He could at least have had the decency to be horrible, since what he made me suffer was horrible. But the French police have always had a particularly humane way of being inhumane. We chatted a little on the stairs, as though he wasn't just about to lock me in a rat-hole without letting me wash, or phone my nearest and dearest, without giving me something to read, with nothing, like a dying dog, like a bundle of dirty laundry; and here I am banged up again politely, the three bolts shooting home on the door of my garbage dump, adorned with the graffiti 'Fuck the Police' and 'Kill the Feds'.

Once again I found myself alone with a shady character who had just been arrested for exhibitionism and shoplifting. I didn't dare ask him whether he had stolen the apples before showing his penis to a customer, or whether he had started by flashing the check-out girl before palming a tin of cassoulet, or whether he committed the crimes simultaneously: it would have taken quite some skill to drop his pants in front of some fiftysomething housewife while relieving her of her purse. Whatever the circumstances, he was drunk and aggressive, constantly hurling abuse at the police; the moment he recognised me he became threatening, demanding that I give him 10,000 euros, screaming out my name so the other prisoners would know who I was, and the others began to chant the name of the TV station I worked for, threatening to kidnap me or to sell the story to the papers. The word 'cocksucker' sprang readily to their lips, like an obsession, a preoccupation, perhaps an unspoken desire.

'I've got a friend who works at the Post Office. Give him two minutes and he'll find your address on the internet. We're going to pay you a little visit.'

I didn't flinch, I said nothing. I curled up in a foetal position on the filthy foam mattress on the floor and pretended to doze amid the dust-balls and dead cockroaches. But I couldn't sleep. I was sorry I had never memorised the hatha yoga mantras of Sri Krishnamacharya, which make it possible to achieve an ascetic state that involves all the strength of mind and body.

# 15

# AFFECTIVE PROGNATHISM

I am living in my childhood, I am settling back into my past.

The only names from my childhood I remember are those of the girls I loved and who never had the faintest idea: Marie-Aline Dehaussy, the Mirailh sisters, Clarence Jacquard, Cécile Favreau, Claire Guionnet, Michèle Luthala, Béatrice Kahn, Agathe Olivier, Axelle Batonnier . . . I think most of them dated my brother, but the periods and places get mixed up . . . My aunt Delphine assures me that the first girl I ever kissed on the lips was Marie-Aline, in a wooden hut on the big beach at Guéthary. For a long time, my mother kept a picture of the two of us arm in arm; we are smiling proudly, our swimming costumes are wet, there is sand in our hair. Her cheeks dimple as she smiles, as do mine. We must be eight or nine; the first kiss on the lips was a major event for me, but what about her? I have no idea. My brother and my aunt sweetly called her 'my fiancée' to make me blush. Was I ever happier than I was on that forgotten day?

I have a better memory of the first girl I ever kissed with my mouth open and got some tongue action. This was much later; I was thirteen, it was at an afternoon party on the rue de Buci. The girl was particularly pretty, but a friend with a Wrangler jacket told me that she was up for a slow dance with me. He pushed her towards me while I bent over to tie the laces of my Kickers, to give my blushes time to subside. She was a blonde girl called Vera, an American my age. When she smiled, I realised why she wasn't put off by the braces on my teeth: she was sporting the same twisted metal bumpers. I put my hands on her shoulders, but she moved them down to her hips; she made all the running. Since the shutters were closed, Vera smelled of perspiration, and the armpits of my Fruit of the Loom T-shirt stank too. Four coloured lights (one red, one green, one blue, one yellow) blinked more or less in time to 'If You Leave Me Now' by Chicago (first snog, standing up) and 'I'm Not in Love' by 10cc (second snog, sitting on the couch). Both songs still make me cry every time I hear them. When they come on the radio, if anyone dares speak to me, change the station, or even thinks of turning down the volume, I become homicidal. I later learned that the boy who introduced Vera and me had ordered her to go out with me because otherwise I would turn out queer – I was on my own in the corner drinking an apple-and-blackcurrant Fruité, staring down at the slice of dried Savane cake on a paper plate, hiding my orthodontic smile as best I could. At thirteen, I was the only boy in my class who had never French kissed. Vera had snogged me to amuse her pals; my first French kiss was the result of a humiliating dare. When I found out, I felt like shit but I was proud all the same to have gone through a rite of passage: to have wrapped my tongue around dental braces other than my own. I boasted about it for at least a week in the playground of the Lycée Montaigne. There were no girls at the Lycée Bossuet, then suddenly, in the *sixième*, I found myself in the co-educational classes of a state school. Up until that party at the rue Buci, I was an oral virgin. At the Lycée Montaigne I discovered what my teenage years were destined to be: a litany of unspoken passions, a mixture of intense pain, diffuse desire, veiled frustration, chronic shyness, a series of silent disappointments, a collection of unrequited loves, of misunderstandings, of ill-timed and futile blushes. My youth would consist mainly of staring at the ceiling of my bedroom listening to 'If You Leave Me Now' and 'I'm Not in Love'.

Another time, I announced in a victorious tone to my brother that I had fondled the breasts of Claire, a pretty girl in my class. Those were my first caresses of a barely budding breast; through a Fiorucci T-shirt, over the top of her bra, I felt the soft, firm curve, the tender swelling, hard in the centre, a round softness near the erect nipple . . . Charles then told me that I was pathetic, that he had fondled Claire's breasts under her T-shirt, after taking off her bra; he had even stroked her skin, Ye gods! . . . Yet again, I was outclassed. My brother was wilder than me in his teens. At sixteen, he was fucking girls on the roof terrace of our house. One time, he took some girl's cherry in our bedroom; I remember the bloody sheets in the morning which worried my mother and magnified my admiration tenfold. I was the shy son and he was the wild one. At some point, he decided to rejoin the ranks, to tame the demon inside him . . . I rushed to take his place.

Nor have I forgotten Clarence Jacquard, a neighbour from the house across the rue Coëtlogon.

I loved her but never said anything. I blushed so much I could not bring myself to speak to her. I turned scarlet when I saw her at the far end of the schoolyard of the Lycée Montaigne, and even when she wasn't there, at the mere mention of her name. All my friends teased me. At night, locked in the bathroom, I taught myself to say her name without blushing. I barely slept. But as soon as I was in school, it came back. All it took was for me to think about her, or for someone to suspect I might be thinking about her, or for me to suspect that someone might suspect that I might possibly be thinking about her, and I would go red as a beetroot. From my bedroom, I would watch her eating dinner alone with her mother in the house across the street. She had dark hair with a fringe, and a long nose. I don't know why I was so enamoured of this neighbour. She and her mother had the same nose: sometimes a simple detail brings forth the most wonderful feeling. Clarence Jacquard knows nothing of my passion. She was everything to me; to her, I was nothing. I never once dared go up to her, I have no idea what has become of her. I am using her real name here, feeling like a grown-up, but if some fortysomething woman comes up to me some day at the Salon du Livre and tells me off for mentioning her name in my latest book, I'm pretty sure that I'll blush again, even if she has grown up to be hideously ugly, which would make it even more embarrassing.

It is from these frequent rejections, these turned cheeks, these childish jealousies, these adolescent frustrations, that my addiction to the lips of women stems. When you have met with such rejection, hoped so much and dared so little, how can you possibly not spend the rest of your life treating every kiss as a victory? I will never manage to get out of my head the notion that any woman who wants me is the most beautiful woman in the world.

It is possible to forget your past. That doesn't mean that you ever get over it.

# 16

# QUIET DAYS IN NEUILLY

I was not abused, or beaten, or taken into care by social services; I am simply the second son of a couple from the south-west of France. I was brought up by my mother after my parents divorced, though I spent one weekend a month and part of the school holidays at my father's place. The register of births, marriages and deaths is categorical: I was born on 21 September 1965, at 2, boulevard du Château, Neuilly-sur-Seine, at 9.05 p.m. After that: nothing. My childhood slips away from me like a dream in the morning: the harder I try to remember it, the more it steals away into the mist.

The world into which I was born has little in common with the world we know today. It was the France that existed before May 1968, still presided over by a General who wore a grey uniform. I am old enough now to have witnessed a whole way of life disappear: a way of speaking, a style of dressing, of wearing one's hair, a world where there was only one TV channel whose flagship programme was a circus spectacular in black and white (*La Piste aux étoiles*). In those days, police officers had pea whistles and carried white truncheons. It was twenty years after Auschwitz and Hiroshima, the sixty-two million dead, the deportations, the Liberation, the hunger, the destitution, the cold. Grown-ups talked about the war, their voices dropping to a whisper whenever children came into the room. They would flinch at noon on the first Thursday of every month when they heard the public warning sirens being tested. Their sole obsession during the years of my childhood was creature comforts. For fifty years after the war, everyone embraced greed. That's why my father chose to pursue a highly lucrative career in business when his true vocation was philosophy.

We walked to my nursery school in Neuilly in single file, holding on to a piece of string. We lived on the ground floor of a *hôtel particulier* on a quiet street lined with palm trees and streetlamps – the rue Saint-James, which was pronounced '*Sinjam*', at number 28. It was a narrow street with no shops and no noise, where even the nannies whispered. Our room overlooked a small garden with rose bushes bordered by a low privet hedge. A tricycle lay overturned on the lawn.

Apparently there was a weeping willow. I've often walked that street since, to see whether my memory might come back: nothing came to me, but still the willow weeps. I hoped some hitherto unseen images might suddenly appear, but I remembered nothing of the lawn on which I took my first steps. I was struck by the tranquillity, the sense of peace this well-heeled street exudes. How had my parents managed to fight in such a quiet thoroughfare? It is a residential lane mimicking a perfect rustic village right in the middle of the suburbs of Paris. You could easily imagine you were in London, near Grosvenor Square, or in the Hamptons, with lawns sloping gently towards the Atlantic (if you substitute the Seine for the ocean). My mother told me she took her babies for walks in a navy-blue pram, with spoked wheels and white tyres, bought at Bonnichon. One day she ran into the actor Pierre Fresnay, who lived next door. 'What beautiful children!' he cried. It was my first encounter with the world of show business. My mother wore a pale-pink tartan mini-kilt; in certain photographs from that period she looks like Nancy Sinatra in the Scopitone – an early form of music videos played on a jukebox – of 'Sugar Town', 1967.*

* 'I've got some troubles but they won't last/I'm gonna lay

My brother and I were dressed in Molli, and later, when we gambolled about, we wore little tweed coats with velvet collars brought back from Harrods in London. But this utopia was not as perfect as our outfits.

Maman had to put up with the fact that her American mother-in-law lived nearby and would turn up out of the blue bringing boxes of After Eight. Her husband's mother lived in the adjacent street (rue Delabordère), but Maman had not yet got to the point of sending her packing when she rang the doorbell to give lectures on how to bring up her grandchildren. Granny was apparently very critical of our nanny, a German woman who had once belonged to the Hitler Youth: Anne-Gret', a charming, very authoritarian lady whose love of discipline had not been diminished one whit by the fall of the Reich. I still have an itchy green image of her: a character dressed from head to foot in coarse Loden cloth. The first words I ever heard were spoken with a German accent. Anne-Gret' had the peculiar habit of licking a handkerchief and giving our faces a cat-lick using her saliva. Back

---

right down here in the grass/And pretty soon all my troubles will pass/Cause I'm in shoo-shoo-shoo-shoo-shoo-sugar town.'

then there were no paper handkerchiefs. The bois de Boulogne had been the favoured park of German officers twenty years previously, but perhaps Anne-Gret' did not know this.

In itself, being born in Neuilly-sur-Seine does not constitute a handicap in life, but the area hardly instils a fighting spirit. One could cross the road in a silence broken only by the chirping of sparrows and the purr of English cars. My pram probably glided beneath the trees in the leafy Jardins de Bagatelle; I know that my brother nearly drowned in Mare Saint-James, having dived in before he had learned how to swim one day when my mother's back was turned, and sometimes I still dream that I am gliding in a boat through this mysterious pink and green forest. The clouds scud past above my head; the tangled branches of the chestnut trees cut the firmament into neat squares and I fall asleep in the lake of the bois de Boulogne, lulled by the splash of oars in the still water. The backdrops of my earliest childhood still exist, and yet when I go back there, they evoke no memories. Only their names seem to hail from a bygone age, a distant country, quaint and long since vanished, a strangely familiar land . . . The artificial rocks of 'La Grande Cascade' remind me of a mysterious grotto, a magical cave hidden behind the thundering waterfall. The restaurant 'Le Pré Catelan' with the horse-drawn carriages lined up outside merges with my memory of coming into the central alley of the Villa Navarre in Pau . . . The Botanical Garden was our paradise, our miniature Disneyland with fairground rides lit up with coloured lights, the call of the monkeys, the smell of dung and of waffle stands . . . The 'Chalet des Îles', a wooden chalet imported from Switzerland and set in a lake, was a planet orbited by white boats like satellites tracing wakes between the swans and the water lilies . . . The 'Hippodrome de Longchamp' with the crowds in their Sunday best, cars honking, the derelict windmill, the tipsters offering advice, the horses passing through the weighing room, a sea of hats and umbrellas . . . The 'Tir aux Pigeons' restaurant with its giant parasols, its starched white table-cloths, its gravel pathways that crunched beneath my baby sandals like broken biscuits . . . Did I truly live these things, or am I performing a historical reconstruction of my own life? In my first three novels, I chose to give my alter ego the name 'Marronnier', as both a corruption of my mother's maiden name and also to pay homage to the chestnut trees in the bois de Boulogne, to the lush green foliage casting shadows like Chinese lanterns, to the chestnut trees in flower along the avenue de Madrid. The 'Polo de Paris', which my father joined in 1969 . . . People joined the 'Polo' to disparage the 'Tir', and joined the 'Tir' to pour scorn on the 'Racing', and the 'Racing' only if they could not secure membership to either of the others, which for the most part meant one was Jewish. The *maîtres d'hôtels* wore white jackets – this was before they built the swimming pool there – and my brother taught me how to make mud pies in the sandpit. We played conkers against what my mother called 'filthy rich kids' to a soundtrack of the dull thwock of tennis balls and the whisper of canvas Spring Court shoes on the ochre clay of the courts . . . An image comes back to me: an Argentinean polo player falling from his horse, the match being suspended, an ambulance driving over the field, nurses clambering out, lifting him onto a stretcher, the ambulance driving away – it was a white Citroën DS estate, the player with the fractured leg was wearing big brown boots . . . White and brown like the colours of the clubhouse, which looks like a house on Long Island. I watch the ambulance through my father's binoculars, though I have turned them the wrong way round, so the car seems smaller and more distant, just like my memories. We ate melon served on a bed of crushed ice, strawberries smothered in thick *crème fraîche* (the fashion for whipped cream comes much later), and we were a little ashamed when Granny cursed in English about the slowness of the service. Coming out of the Polo Club, I would turn and look through the rear windscreen of the Bentley to admire the Trianon de Bagatelle, and the 1920 château, long and squat, with its strange crenellated tower like the one at the Château de Vaugoubert, a medieval vision melting in the grey rain . . . Nowadays in the Parc de Bagatelle, mobile phones ring, dirt bikes roar, teenagers shout, playing football on the lawns, families grill *merguez* on barbecues and ghetto-blasters blare out Britney Spears's 'Womanizer' at top volume. These days, going there in a vintage English car is considered pretentious; forty years ago the bois de Boulogne was exactly as Proust depicted it at the turn of the century. I have often been there since, for night-time car rallies, for tennis matches, for blow-jobs from trans-sexuals. The *bois* no longer has the charm it did in the 1960s: there were no drag artists in the back of my father's high-roofed grey car, instead there were running boards, a mahogany dash, Joan Baez and the scent of old leather. And, sitting in the back next to his big brother, a rather too sheltered boy like a goldfish in its bowl.

Between 1965 and 1970, nothing happened in my life. Neuilly was a little like Geneva, a town that was too clean, where the air was too pure with boredom as the accepted trade-off for feeling protected. Neuilly is a town where time is content simply to pass. How can I describe the mute suffering of the Hauts-de-Seine without sounding preposterous . . .? The *commissaire* at the 8th arrondissement police station was right: my complaint was inexplicable. We lived in the only respectable area, the one near the bois de Boulogne. Neuilly-sur-Seine divides into two distinct towns: as you head down the avenue Charles-de-Gaulle towards La Défense, chic Neuilly is on your left while low-rent Neuilly is on your right, near the town hall. The houses nearest the bois de Boulogne have a certain cachet; the bourgeoisie has a discreet charm, why whine about having been born there? Because that world has disappeared, it has exploded into a thousand shards, because we didn't know our luck, because such a fairy tale could not possibly last. If, with hindsight, I scoff at such indulgence, it is perhaps so that I do not miss what has vanished and gone.

I was born into a closed world, a well-heeled ghetto where gardens were surrounded by hedges pruned with secateurs by gardeners wearing overalls, where we had lunch surrounded by white fences and were not allowed to speak or to put our elbows on the table. Our four o'clock *goûter* was served by Anne-Gret', who would appear in the living room in apron and smock: either 'chocolatines' (as *pains au chocolat* are called by people from the Béarn) which we dunked in glasses of milk until they became flaccid sponges, or squares of Poulain chocolate sandwiched between hunks of Vienna bread which we bit into, often leaving a tooth behind in the process. At the time, Nutella had not yet arrived from Italy, but sometimes we would eat buttered baguettes sprinkled with Benco drinking-chocolate powder. It had something of the atmosphere of Vittorio de Sica's *The Garden of the Finzi-Continis* (1970), all walled estates and languid tennis games. De Sica's film describes the rise of fascism and how a family is destroyed by the war. Our destruction, which happened twenty years later, came in May 1968 with the massive student protests which my parents prided themselves on going to see, driving down to l'Odéon in the grey Bentley, little knowing that this wind of change would overwhelm them and bring about their separation.

There is something more difficult than becoming bourgeois, and that is losing one's status – a phrase I prefer to the tasteless word 'decline'. How does one shake off the refined education, the preposterous ideas, the prejudices, the neuroses, the guilt, the self-consciousness, the side parting, the itchy poloneck jumpers, the blazers with their gilt buttons, the scratchy grey-flannel trousers with the knife-edge crease, the smugness, the snobby accent and the lies? You lose your memory. The French state claims to do everything possible so that people can rise through the social ranks, but no help is offered when they fall. In the face of ruin, amnesia is the only refuge of the well-heeled. My father generously did everything in his power to prevent his children from suffering as a result when the Villa Navarre, the sanatorium in Béarn, went bankrupt in the late 1970s. But he didn't succeed in hiding from us the dire straits of our family, which in former times had been the richest in Pau. The death of my grandparents and the ensuing squabbles over property pervaded my childhood and ruined my adolescence. I remember an appalling question my maternal great-grandmother is supposed to have asked when first introduced to my father at the Château de Vaugoubert: 'What's his birth?' On the day they were introduced the Comtesse de Chasteigner subjected him to her famous '*foie gras* test': the chambermaid brought several slices on a plate; they had to be eaten using a fork, and not spread on bread on pain of being permanently pigeon-holed as plebeian. Having been alerted beforehand by my mother, Jean-Michel Beigbeder passed the test with flying colours . . .

Scarcely fifteen years later, we were bankrupt. The Beigbeder family shifted from one way of life to another, from the position of country squires rooted in an illusory eternity, like the trees in the grounds of the Villa Navarre, to that of modern neo-bourgeois, rootless, urban, ephemeral and pressured – pressured because aware just how precarious our position was. Leaving Neuilly for the 16th arrondissement in Paris, we moved into a swiftness devoid of memory, the haste of those who have no time to lose; or rather: we invented a new bourgeoisie who could no longer afford the luxury of searching for lost time.

It is difficult to recover from an unhappy childhood, but to recover from a sheltered childhood may be impossible.

# 17

# A CLAUSTROPHOBIC CHAPTER

'I'm warning you, if you don't release me right now, I'll write a book!'

I ended up becoming as belligerent as my cellmates. All the others arrested that night were released the following morning, except for a kid who had knocked over a moped in front of a police car. He keeps telling me, 'You're looking at being here for quite a while . . .' Thanks for cheering me up. He puts his head in his hands; he's frantic because he is going to arrive late for work and might well lose his job. I feel like I've been alone here in this shithole for a hundred years, forgotten forever. A uniformed official brings us plastic trays of Basquaise chicken and rice that smells of fish. The chicken was probably bred in an aquarium and fed on plankton. I don't know what time it is: eleven o'clock, maybe noon. My rumpled clothes disgust me. I start to pray: I recite the Our Father, the Hail Mary, not out of any sense of piety but because it can't hurt and it means I don't have to think. The worst thing is thinking about the people I love; withdrawal gnaws at me, and the fact that they might be worried. I discover the horror of being a prisoner, which turns you into a pressure cooker. I have to make a superhuman effort not to think about the existence of an outside world where people can come and go as they please. I can feel myself cracking up, and struggle not to fall apart. A few minutes later I realise that claustrophobic tears have trickled down my cheeks. I'm not exactly Tony Montana, with my quivering chin and my tear-soaked beard. I'm the sort of person who can cry at the drop of a hat: for example, every time my daughter bursts into tears in front of me, I do likewise, which is hardly the best way to comfort her. The most preposterous reconciliation in some third-rate soap opera can turn me into a gasping, spluttering baby; it's pathetic. I didn't know until now that I suffered from claustrophobia. But this enforced spell in the dungeons reminds me of the couple of times I've suffered acute panic attacks: once while visiting the caves of Sare (terror, sweaty temples, which steadily increased the farther we moved from the entrance to the cave – apparently people experience the same thing visiting the pyramids in Egypt), the other time going to a Goth concert in the catacombs of Paris (we had to crawl through a dark, damp, narrow passageway to get to an underground room covered in graffiti, and I suddenly had the feeling of being buried alive, a taste of ashes in my mouth. I have to stop thinking about it even now or it will bring on an attack of tachycardia). Right now, as with both of these episodes, I start suffocating at the thought that I can't get out into the open air immediately. Claustrophobia is drowning without water, a combination of asphyxia and panic. The fear of suffocation is suffocating the way the fear of blushing makes you blush. The nagging question that haunts the claustrophobe, that eats away at his nerves, is: How can I accept the fact that I am here AGAINST MY WILL? The prisoner is an unwitting nomad. When incarcerated, he discovers he was born to be a backpacker. In custody, he contemplates suicide, but how can he kill himself? He has been left with no sharp objects, no rope, no belt, no laces with which to strangle himself. Even the strip lights in the ceiling are protected by metal grilles to prevent any attempt at electrocution. He could beat his head against the floor, but, as he is constantly watched by CCTV cameras, the duty officers would probably get there in time; he would probably end up with a broken nose, a split eyebrow and a longer period in custody while his injuries were treated in the infirmary.

Outside my cell, I notice a folding shelf mounted in the corridor, supported by two metal bars. I could just get my head between the two flaps. All I would have to do is ask to be let out to go for a piss, and hurl myself at this rough and ready garrotte. If I quickly put my head in the hole and swiftly turned it 180 degrees, I could break my neck, I would be strangled, hanged fifty centimetres off the ground; it would require only a moment's inattention, the screw would not have time to react. But there's nothing to say I wouldn't end up quadriplegic. I might spend the rest of my life in a wheelchair dictating my books by blinking my left eyelid, like Jean-Dominique Bauby, the journalist who first hired me to work for *Elle* in 1997. The elegance with which he described his ordeal restores my confidence a little. A line from his book *The Diving Bell and the Butterfly* comes back to me: 'If I must drool, I may as well drool on cashmere.' Who am I to think about suicide after one night in the cells? It's not exactly as serious as being a prisoner of a body transformed into a diving bell. I take a deep breath to dispel my panic. I try to count the seconds the way I used to count sheep to get to sleep, before I was old enough to start taking Stilnox every night. I reel off the list of phone numbers I know by heart, the list of books I've read this year, the TV programmes day by day. The feeling of imprisonment is absolute torture, probably akin to Chinese water torture. Time expands, freedom seems like a faint light at the end of an endless tunnel, a glow growing ever more distant, like the camera shot invented by Hitchcock in *Vertigo*: the 'dolly zoom'. To suggest the vertigo suffered by the hero, played by James Stewart, the camera pulls back and at the same time zooms in, so that the stairwell stretches and the image becomes distorted. James Stewart has vertigo, and I am James Stewart. My body is overcome by a new wave of sadness; isolated, abandoned, I feel as though no one will come to my rescue, that I have been forgotten here, beneath the earth, for centuries. Thousands of bolts and locks separate me from the outside world. And I have only been in custody for twelve hours. I cannot bring myself to imagine what long-term prisoners must feel. When I was on a jury at the *cours d'assises* in Paris, I blithely sent rapists and murderers to prison for eight, ten, twelve years. I would be more tolerant now. Every citizen summoned to appear on a jury should have to spend a short period behind bars so that they know what they will be inflicting on the accused. In custody, the human brain goes into overdrive; you fantasise, have nightmares, go round in circles until you think you're going insane. You need to summon the strength of will to become a Benedictine monk in the blink of an eye. To renounce the world, withdraw into yourself, cut yourself off from all desires. Nobly accept your fate. Rid yourself of all curiosity, all existential questioning, become a house plant. I'm painfully aware that this whole thing is ridiculous, that I'm just a privileged child deprived of his comforts as punishment for his overgrown-rich-kid self-indulgence. Do not dismiss my suffering; comfort has been the great struggle of the French ever since the Liberation. This thing we call freedom is chiefly a struggle for a cushier existence than that of earlier generations. Seen in this light, my pain is not quite so contemptible; if you think about it, human comfort is about the only progress made in the twentieth century. Comfort is oblivion in a Parker-Knoll armchair.

Some day, prisons will all be converted into museums of suffering which our grandchildren will look upon with horror and incomprehension, like Alcatraz Penitentiary in San Francisco Bay, which I toured with my father and my brother when I was ten – and there you go, another memory has come back to me. In 1975, the most famous prison in the world was an island surrounded by shark-infested waters. Since it closed, it has been possible to visit it the way you might one of the châteaux in the Loire. The sky was orange that day, like the rusty cell bars and the Golden Gate Bridge. We took a ferry. Forrest Mars, owner of the company that produced Mars bars, had organised a trip to the United States for my father and his two sons. 'The Alcatraz Tour', according to the brochure. We followed a guide dressed as a warder who told us horrible stories and showed us the thick bars on the cell windows, the yard where the convicts exercised, the cell where Al Capone did his time, the dank dungeons where recalcitrant prisoners were banged up in the dark, the thickness of the walls; he told us about the punishments, the escape attempts that inevitably ended in drowning or in a shark feast. That night, in our room at the Fairmont Hotel, Charles and I had nightmares while Papa snored next door.

Hit a writer on the head and nothing comes out. Bang him up and he recovers his memory.

# 18

# DIVORCE, FRENCH-STYLE

I write the word 'divorce', but for years my parents never so much as uttered the word. It was like the 'events' in Algeria; during the Fifth Republic, rhetoric made immoderate use of litotes; even Georges Pompidou's cancer was unmentionable. The subject of my parents' separation was brushed under the carpet, evaded, toned down, obliterated; my mother would answer her sons' questions by saying, 'Your father is away on business,' long before Kusturica's film used the title, and photos of them together still took pride of place in the living room of our apartment in the 16th arrondissement as though nothing had changed. Reality was denied; my mother wanted us to believe that everything was normal and that we should not worry about the almost permanent absence of our father in the early 1970s. In those days, women's magazines probably advised against telling young children the truth. Françoise Dolto had not yet published her groundbreaking book on infant psychology *La Cause des enfants*; babies were not yet people. Out of kindness, my mother took it upon herself to remain dignified and silent on the subject. Divorce was a non-subject. My father became The Invisible Man (as played by David McCallum in the TV series of the period). We eventually worked out that our father had left us for his job, that he worked day and night at the office and spent the whole year travelling. I don't remember the avenue Henri-Martin, the dark-brown duplex apartment wallpapered with Japanese 'Nobilis' paper, though it was here I obsessively watched a cartoon called *Les Shadoks* from 1969 to 1972. My only memory, strangely, is of an act of rebellion which probably happened that same year. Our parents had taken my brother and me out in my father's green Rover. The car was speeding silently down the motorway. My father was very tense, it was raining, my mother said nothing and we could hear only the rasp of the windscreen wipers punctuating the silence like the brush-beat of a jazz drummer. I was staring at the side window, at the raindrops streaking backwards as though fleeing the sickly smell of the beige leather seats. That smell of vintage English car leather is forever associated in my mind with the vanished years that followed my parents' divorce. Every time I get into a car that smells of dead cow, I have to stop myself from retching. My father finally parked the hulking car outside a huge red-brick building on which was engraved the name 'Passy-Buzenval' (Maman thought the name sounded like 'Buchenwald'). Charles and I were terrified: the place looked like a prison. Which in fact is what it was: my father had decided to enrol us in this Catholic boarding school in Reuil-Malmaison, not as punishment perhaps but to keep us away from our mother's lover, to put us out to pasture, to shelter us from the divorce or I don't know what; but as soon as we got out of the car he clearly realised the absurdity of the idea. Not long before this, my mother had tried to sign me up for cub scouts, and I had run away.

My father muttered, 'Oh look, they have tennis courts and a swimming pool.'

At which point my brother, who was eight years old, spoke up and calmly said, 'If you enrol us here we'll run away as soon as it gets dark, we'll escape, we'll leave the first night, we will never sleep in this place.'

I think that my father moved from nervousness to fear. Now, I realise he must have been imagining his nightmarish childhood as a boarding pupil at the Abbaye de Sorèze. My parents cut short the guided tour of the school. A crowd of boarders had gathered around the Rover and they parted to allow us to drive off. The drive back was less silent than the drive there, and much more cheerful: we all burst out laughing listening to Albert Simon read the weather report on Europe Numéro Un. He had a shrill, quavering voice and mangled his Rs: 'Stwong wisk of vawiable weather along the Meditewwanean . . .' Then Papa reached over to the dashboard and shoved in the eight-track cartridge of *Rubber Soul*, the best album by the Beatles, who had also just split up, and we all sang 'Baby you can drive my car, and baby I love you, beep-beep yeah,' bobbing our heads like the nuclear family we no longer were. It had been a close call. Maman moved to the 6th arrondissement and enrolled us at the École Bossuet. That day, the drive chain of family misfortune jammed, thanks to the rebellion of Charles, my saviour.

I also know, because my mother told me, that around the time my parents separated, I began to get nosebleeds. I had contracted an innocuous illness known as 'epistaxis': the blood vessels in my nostrils were very fragile; I was almost a haemophiliac. All my shirts were bloodstained, a scarlet fountain spurted daily from my face, I swallowed a lot of haemoglobin and vomited quite a lot too. It was quite spectacular, since I became very pale from all these nosebleeds. My daughter Chloë is terrified of blood, and I don't dare tell her I grew up spattered in the stuff, in red-stained pyjamas, that I would sometimes wake up lying in the sticky dampness of a pillow that was completely saturated. Auto-vampiric, I grew accustomed to the salty taste that daily trickled down my throat. I swallowed litres of a red liquid that was not wine. I had perfected an infallible technique for stopping my nosebleeds (pinch the nostrils for five minutes without lowering my head while waiting for the blood to coagulate) or triggering them (with a quick blow to the bridge of the nose, or by picking at the scab inside the nostril), and blood would flow, forming large pools on the kitchen floor or in my bathroom washbasin, red suns against white porcelain. 'This cup is my blood, which is shed for you.' After a whole week of constant nosebleeds which I had triggered for a laugh, on a whim, or because of a need for attention, my mother, guilt-stricken about the effects of the divorce proceedings which were going on, drove me in the lashing rain to the Hôpital des Enfants Malades to see Professor Vialatte, an eminent paediatric consultant. This bigwig further terrified her by suggesting it might be the onset of anaemia, refused to rule out leukaemia, and finally recommended complete rest somewhere by the sea.

Hence my first memory: Guéthary 1972 has become my Rosetta Stone, my Promised Land, my Neverland, the secret code of my childhood, my Atlantis, a glimmer from down the ages like those stars which have been dead for thousands of years and yet still twinkle, bringing us news from the edges of the universe and the far end of time.

In Guéthary in 1972, I was still intact. If this book were a DVD, at this point I would press PAUSE, to freeze this image forever. My utopia is behind me.

# 19

## VAN VOGT'S 'NULL-A' AND FRED'S 'A'

My childhood needs to be reinvented: childhood is a novel.

France is an amnesiac nation; my lack of memory is irrefutable proof of my nationality.

Amnesia is a lie of omission. Time is a camera, sending pictures flashing before our eyes. The only way to know what happened in my life between 21 September 1965 and 21 September 1980 is to invent it. It's possible that I thought I was amnesiac when actually I was just a lazy bastard with no imagination. Nabokov and Borges have much the same thing to say: imagination is a form of memory.

When I get out of here, I'll flick through my mother's photo albums as Annie Ernaux does in *Les Années*. Those yellowed images which prove that my life did, after all, begin somewhere. On a photo taken in the gardens of the Villa Patrakénéa in Guéthary, my brother and I are identically dressed: blue-and-white-striped polo-neck sweaters with buttons at the throat, grey Bermuda shorts, Kickers on our feet bought from Western House on the rue des Cannettes. When you spend your whole childhood dressed in the same clothes as your brother, you spend all your adulthood trying to differentiate yourself from him. I had a side parting like the one the young guitarists in French rock bands have these days. My floppy blond fringe was thirty years ahead of its time. I used to buy yellow Malabar bubblegum at ten centimes a piece from the kiosk on the main beach, lick my wrist and apply the transfer tattoos that came free inside. I was that tow-headed little boy who smelled of Bien-Être cologne and wore lederhosen, playing in the grounds of the Villa Navarre or the Château de Vaugoubert in Quinsac. In a pair of red corduroy jeans, I scrabbled up the steep beech trees of the Iraty forest, rolled down the corresponding soft valleys, and spewed up the macaroons from Chez Adam and the hot chocolate from Dodin in the Aston Martin driving us home. Four-wheel drive did not exist back then, and at every bend we kids would be tossed around on the back seat of Father's new car. I got soaked in the cold water of a river beneath towering fir trees where the air was pervaded by the smell of pine resin. I posed with my brother in front of a flock of ewes that smelled of the cheese made from their milk. The meadows were varnished by a curtain of rain, the cloudy skies were a sleepy eiderdown, time passed slowly; as children we hated walks, I think we were as gloomy as our rubber boots were muddy while Pottok ponies passed on the verdant slopes of Zugarramurdi. Every Sunday in summer in Guéthary church, drunk on incense, I would sing hymns in Basque: *'Jainkoaren bildotcha zukensen duzu mundunko bekatua emaguzu bakea'* (Lamb of God who takes away the sins of the world, have mercy upon us). I hope my Basque friends will forgive me if the spelling is approximate . . . Holed up in this cell, I don't have a missal to check, so I'm quoting from memory, given that for once I've actually remembered something. I slipped on the diving board in the swimming pool at the Hôtel du Palais in Biarritz, and when it came to stitching the gaping wound without anaesthetic, my mother says I was stoic. I was proud of my childhood bravery, as the scar on my chin still attests. I owned a record player on which I played singles by the group Il Était une Fois, by Joe Dassin,

Nino Ferrer or Mike Brant. The singer with Il Était une Fois died of an overdose, as did Joe Dassin, while Mike Brant and Nino Ferrer both committed suicide. It's possible to say that from an early age my cultural tastes were *marginal*. I wore slobbery pink dental braces on my teeth that hooked over my canines with elastic bands and had metal rings held together with wire that dug into my gums. On the ancient staircases at both Pau and Guéthary I smelled the same odour of floor wax, but that fragrance also reminds me of Sare, where my grandfather had bought another house: I would watch the cows sleeping in the hazy meadows of the Spanish mountain, I would take the little train that climbed to the summit of La Rhune. To this day, it is the most beautiful landscape I have ever seen, and I have travelled a lot since then. The cows were beige or black and every possible nuance of green was visible beneath the blue of the sky, the white blotches were flocks of sheep; try as it might, the eye could not find any ugliness, at every point of the compass this mountain was filled with joy. I travelled with my brother and my father, in America and Asia, to the Antilles, to Indonesia, Mauritius and the Seychelles. It was on one of these exotic holidays that something critical happened: I started to write, though at the time

I could barely read. There are copybooks somewhere in which I began recording all our activities. Unfortunately, I lost these key pieces of evidence. Where is the Clairefontaine exercise book in which I wrote for the first time . . .? It was in Bali in 1974 that I began my career as an autobiographer. Our father had taken us to Indonesia for a month: a great and beautiful trip that I would remember nothing about were it not all meticulously written down in a notebook. It was there that I first contracted this preposterous habit: day after day, I would jot down everything I had done, what we ate, the beaches, the sights, the Balinese folk dancing in traditional costumes (crooked fingers, tilted heads, long fingernails, arched feet, golden-pointed headdresses like temples), the fights with my brother in the pool, the endless procession of my father's girlfriends, Charles being unable to climb out of the water in his water-skiing suit and the earthquake that woke us up one night in the Hotel Tandjung Sari and the snake that Charles spotted in the sea at Kuta Beach which turned out to be the shadow of his snorkel. My father told us that the sea was infested with 'minute snakes', so named because anyone who stepped on them would die a minute later. And then he was surprised that we refused to swim anywhere but in the hotel swimming pool! Why, when I never felt the need before, did I suddenly have the urge to set down my whole life in double-spaced copy-books? Probably because even then I realised that writing was a means of remembering. I became a punctilious scribe of the ephemeral, an alchemist capable of transforming a month-long holiday into an eternity. I wrote to capture fleeting moments. This is why I only wrote during holidays with my father – the following summer, I had the same urge on our American tour. If I've forgotten everything, perhaps it is because my memory was contained within these child-hood notebooks.

And then came my first hour of glory: appearing on television with the Bogdanoff Brothers. In 1979 I was a little blond boy with a voice like a girl, who, live on their programme *Temps X*, declared that 'Science fiction is the prognostic research of the possible.' The Russian twins in their space suits were regular visitors to my father's cocktail parties; at his house, they always saw me with my nose in novels of space opera or the monthly cyberpunk comic *Métal Hurlant*, which was why they invited me to come on the programme to talk about post-atomic 'geek' culture. The TF1 studios on the rue Cognacq-Jay looked like a flying saucer made of asbestos. The following Monday at the Lycée Bossuet I savoured the jealousy of my classmates and the respect of Father di Falco, the headmaster. By appearing on television, I had become the headmaster's pet: he offered me a 45 rpm single to which he had penned the lyrics: 'Father Christmas, do you really exist?'

I had got into science fiction thanks to les Éditions Gallimard, who had launched a collection of children's books called '1,000 Soleils' which republished Ray Bradbury's *The Martian Chronicles* and *Fahrenheit 451*, as well as *The Strange Case of Dr Jekyll and Mr Hyde* by Robert Louis Stevenson. This made a startling change from my previous reading matter: the boy's own series 'Signes de Piste'! Gallimard also published classics by H.G. Wells: *The War of the Worlds, The Invisible Man* and *The Time Machine* . . . in fact, I'm travelling in that time machine right now. The covers were drawn by Enki Bilal. Later, my father suggested I read Barjavel's *The Ice People*, which was a profoundly erotic shock. For a long time, Eléa, the frozen blonde discovered buried in ice around the South Pole, was my ideal woman; nothing arouses me more than the prospect of thawing a frigid blonde. I read everything Barjavel ever wrote: *Ashes, Ashes*; *Future Times*

*Three* – another great novel about time travel, something I was by now obsessed with. I read nothing but science fiction: I collected the series 'Présence du Futur', I devoured Asimov's Robot books and, most importantly, A.E. van Vogt's Null-A saga (both published by J'ai Lu), which my brother had dog-eared before me. Charles loved science fiction too: he collected futuristic comics – *Valérian*, *Yoko Tsuno*, *Blake and Mortimer* – and was fascinated by astronomy, by galaxies and distant planets. Perhaps he too needed to escape. I deeply identified with the non-Aristotelians in van Vogt's *The World of Null-A*, the 1948 novel translated by Boris Vian. The principle is simple: the hero, Gilbert Gosseyn, realises that the town he lives in is not his own, his wife is not his own, that his whole memory is an artifice and he is not who he believed himself to be. The idea has been routinely plagiarised since (most recently in *The Matrix*, Harry Potter and *The Chronicles of Narnia*). It is an extraordinary fantasy for a child: believing that his life is not his own, his parents are not his parents, that his big brother is actually an alien, that his real teachers are elsewhere, that appearances lie, that our senses prove nothing. Only now do I realise how much reading these books was an escape. All through my childhood I dreamed of being a hologram like the ones I had seen in the Haunted House in Disneyland during our trip to California in 1975. My favourite comic was *Philémon* by Fred. I had every volume in the series. They told the story of a little boy who lives on the A in 'Atlantic Ocean'. The letters that appear on maps and globes exist in another dimension as islands in the shape of letters; his father is sceptical and never believes Philémon when he tells him tales of his voyages to 'O.C.É.A.N A.T.L.A.N.T.I.Q.U.E'. I suspect that a lot of children of divorced parents develop this obsession with illusion akin to schizophrenia. They long for a parallel universe more hospitable than this one. Or, subconsciously, they suspect that they are not being told the whole truth. If I lost my memory as an adult, it is perhaps because even when I was young I had little faith in reality. Van Vogt's 'Null-A' and Fred's 'A' are to blame. I met Fred last year at the funeral of Gérard Lauzier in Saint-Germain-des-Prés. I was happy to be able to tell him that, to my mind, he is the French equivalent of Lewis Carroll.

Science fiction led on to hardboiled detective fiction. The themes were often the same: investigations, chase sequences, the search for identity, redemption . . . Substitute grey trenchcoats for spacesuits and Jack Daniel's for Huxley's soma and you've transformed sci-fi into *noir* fiction. I had a penchant for James Hadley Chase, although the covers of the SAS series, which invariably featured scantily clad women, intrigued me for other reasons! The funniest writer was Carter Brown: a spare writing style, rapid-fire dialogue, succinct descriptions and lots of swear-words. One day, my uncle Denis Manuel, seeing I was reading Carter Brown, gave me a piece of advice that was to change my life. Clutching a glass of scotch, he said: 'Read the Commissaire San-Antonio series. It's the only thing I read now, everything else bores me rigid. Stop reading translations and start reading someone who speaks your language. Who cares about the plots? It's the language that matters.' I had a lot of respect for Uncle Denis, who I considered the smartest guy in our family, with his deadpan sense of humour, his cigars and the way he copied JFK's slight stoop. Charles Beigbeder Snr believed in literature, but he had not lived long enough to instil his passion in me; as for my father, he would not read modern novels: as far as he was concerned, literature ended with Dickens and Roger Martin du Gard. He set the bar too high, and had neither the means nor the desire to change it. This had been triggered by the first husband of my aunt and godmother, Nathalie de Chasteigner.

I rushed to the nearest newsagent's in Guéthary, and on a carousel display I found a San-Antonio novel called *Baise-Ball à La Baule*. It was like a firework display! The wild digressions, the terrible puns, the jibes about Jean d'Ormesson, Robert Hossein or François Mitterrand, the verbal frenzy of Inspector Bérurier, the hilarious, obscene, iconoclastic characters – everything about the book was improbable, and yet it sounded true, real, human. Denis was right: in a novel, the plot is a pretext, a canvas; what is important is the man we sense behind the words, the person speaking to us. To this day, I have never heard a better definition of what literature provides: a human voice. The point is not to tell a story; the characters make it possible to listen to someone else, someone who might be my brother, my neighbour, my friend, my ancestor, my double. In 1979, San-Antonio led on to Antoine Blondin who led to Céline, Céline to Rabelais and thereby the whole universe. A world opened up, a parallel galaxy I could access from my bedroom. Can you see the dangerous route by which I came to be a reader of the literary far-right like my grandfather without ever having discussed it with him? Purely and simply because books by these authors were much more entertaining than the stolid works of Camus and Sartre (though incidentally, that is not true: viz. *Words* and *The Fall*). I am sorry that Denis Manuel died of lung cancer at the age of forty-five; I never got to thank him for changing my life. He is also to blame for all my fears: he infected me with a virus from which one never recovers. The joy of being cut off from the world, this was my first addiction. To give up reading novels requires tremendous willpower. You have to want to live, to run, to grow up. I was a drug addict long before I was allowed out at night. I cared more about books than I did about life.

Since that time, I have constantly used reading as a means of making time vanish and writing as a way of holding it back.

# 20

## MADAME RATEL PAINTS

Obviously, one of the most damning pieces of evidence of my childhood is a portrait of me at the age of nine painted by Madame Ratel. In 1974, my father commissioned her to paint a watercolour of each of his sons. Since he saw us less often now, this was a way for him to keep an eye on us. And so, every Thursday afternoon for several weeks my mother drove us to Nicole Ratel's house on the rue Jean-Mermoz to pose in front of her easel and her paintbrushes, sitting on two stools in a vast, murky apartment decorated with cobwebs. She would offer us stale biscuits from a tin box and flat Coke. These sessions posing were long and painful; she began with pencil sketches, then slowly added colour as the glass of water gradually turned as brown as cold coffee. We had to sit up straight and we weren't allowed to play or to leave the room; we had to allow ourselves to be immortalised by the artist, and, not being as narcissistic as I am today, I have to confess that I had rarely been as fucking bored as I was sitting on that stool. I can't precisely remember Madame Ratel's face, but my memory is of something wrinkled and sad with hair in a tight grey bun like Norman Bates's mother in *Psycho*. My memory has transformed her into a cross between a ghost and a witch. The watercolour of my face at the age of nine is reproduced on the facing page of this book: I was once that little blond cherub. My nose and my chin had not yet distorted my face, I did not yet have the dark circles that now make my eyes look sunken, or the beard that hides my pelican's goitre. Only my eyes have not changed, and even then my gaze these days is less candid than in this painting which now hangs in the stairwell of my little house in Paris. Sometimes, when I come home late, he looks at me, seems to judge me. This angelic little boy contemplates his own decline with alarm. Sometimes, when I am very inebriated, I've been known to insult the good little boy who stares down at me from my wall, proud of his age, contemptuous of what I have done with his future:

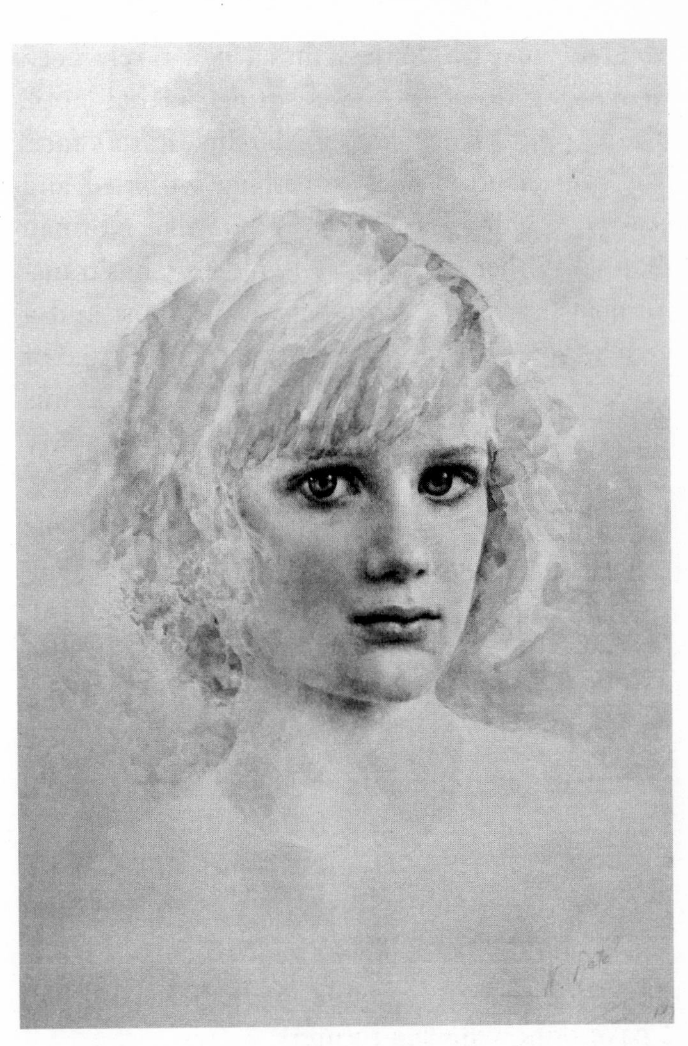

'Hey, you little Pyrenean dipshit! Stop staring at me like that! You're not even ten years old, you live in a little flat with your divorced mother, you're in Year Five in a primary school run by priests, you sleep in the same room as your big brother, you collect the free gadgets that come with *Pif* magazine. You should be proud of the man that you've become! I made all your dreams come true, you snot-nosed brat. You're a writer now, you should admire me instead of looking down your nose at me!'

No answer: watercolours have an arrogant reticence.

'Who the fuck do you think you are?'

'You.'

'And do I really disappoint you as much as that?'

'It's just that thirty years from now I don't want to smell like a wino and be talking to paintings.'

'How dare you judge me! What the fuck do you want? Go on, tell me! I'M JUST AN OLDER YOU! We're the same man, for fuck's sake!'

'You mean the same child?'

The little boy does not blink. It must be my own voice I heard asking the questions, giving the answers – the state I'm in, everything's muddled. My past is staring at me pityingly. I slump down on the stairs. Madame Ratel's portrait maintains a fretful silence, a freshness besotted with absolutes; it is the anti-picture of Dorian Gray, forever flawless, perfect, the eternal witness to my decline, and I stumble before it, I am the one who grows old, who grimaces and frightens. I rush into the kitchen and pour myself a drink, and I raise my glass to this too-pretty boy who I once was, who I do not remember, who will never change.

A few weeks after painting this portrait, Madame Ratel told her husband she loved another man and asked for a divorce. Her husband was less 'laid-back' than my father: the former military officer, who was personnel director for Péchiney in Lacq, drove back to Paris, got his hunting rifle, and at point-blank range he put a bullet through her head before putting the barrel in his mouth. It was their son Stéphane who discovered the carnage when he got home. I think about this man, who must be about the same age as I am now. When I am tempted to bitch about my childhood, I have only to compare it to his to feel like a fool.

Perhaps this is why I dare not sketch out my childhood: the last person to paint my portrait was murdered.

# 21

# FORGOTTEN FINGER

One evening, I left the Polo Club to fetch a tennis ball I'd hit out of the court. I was wearing shorts and a white polo shirt and was clutching my racquet. Suddenly, a young man leaning against a tree called to me: 'Hey, kid, come take a look at my dolly. She's pretty, isn't she?'

The guy opened his black coat and, looking down, I saw a sort of limp pink finger between his legs with two purple wrinkled prunes dangling either side.

'You like her, don't you? Go on, take a good look . . .'

At the time, I didn't say a word; I picked up my ball, turned on my heel and hurried back. I truly believe my Donnay racquet saved me: the guy did not come near me because he thought I might give his wedding tackle a backhand topspin volley, when in fact I was completely petrified. I went back to my tennis lesson as though nothing had happened. Until this moment, I have never mentioned that encounter to anyone. It was not until a few minutes later that my legs started to give out; I had trouble running up to the net. I was ten years old, but this was not the first time I had seen a stranger's cock. In the changing rooms of the Polo Club, adults walked around stark naked in front of the kids; you could see pricks of every size and colour going into or coming out of the showers: I can, for example, attest that the famous publisher Jean-Luc Lagardère was very well endowed. A number of shorter but no less famous penises shrivelled in the changing rooms; I will refrain from naming their owners out of Christian charity. This did not shock me; if men's changing rooms were likely to traumatise children, you would have to ban sport, or ban hygiene. The exhibitionist in the Bagatelle gardens was different: this was the first adult who did not want to protect me. Showing me his cock was certainly a form of aggression, though less serious than using it; thinking about it now, I couldn't care less about the incident, but it is true that it happened. It is strange that this forgotten memory should resurface just as I am going through my story. Maybe it is because, in my turn, the police ordered me to drop my pants.

On the subject of amnesia, one movie that deals with the subject in a very original way is *Men in Black* directed by Barry Sonnenfeld (1997). In this science fiction film, two very special agents 'flash' citizens in order to erase their memories of aliens. After every mission, they take out a large chrome tube, the *neuralyzer*, and the flash dazzles those present, making them lose their memory. I wonder whether my amnesia was not caused in the same way: I saw an alien that I had to forget I'd seen, and in the process I must have 'flashed' all the rest. This is all the more bizarre, since the verb 'to flash' also means to expose oneself in public. The past is made up of successive strata, our memory is a *millefeuille* . . . My shrink reckons this memory is important. I don't, I simply find it trite and repulsive. I set it down here with the others in order of appearance. In doing so, I am aware that I am doing the same thing as the flasher in Bagatelle, the Man in Black who may have wiped out ten years of my life. I am publicly exposing my amnesia.

# 22

# RETURN TO GUÉTHARY

If time must be slowed down, we might as well settle comfortably by the seaside, as one might settle into an armchair. From the depths of my narrow cell, I return to the beach at Cénitz. That afternoon when I was alone with my grandfather at the age of seven is the eye of my hurricane. My parents were overwhelmed, they were too young, too busy being in love, not being in love, too busy making a success or a mess of their lives. Only grandparents can afford the luxury of looking after others. The grassy cliff dropped down towards the sea. The television mast for Rhune served as a lightning rod for the whole coast. The countryside rolled away beneath a golden sky like something out of Turner. On the beach, I picked up pieces of broken bottles that the tides had transformed into transparent green pebbles. My aunt Delphine collected them in a vase: my crop would go to supplement her treasures. At low tide, Cénitz is a rocky beach to which seagulls and 'summer visitors' flocked; they flock there still. The rocks closest to the sand are smooth, but moving towards the sea, they begin to prick the soles of your feet and their slippery seaweed turns them into dangerous ice rinks. You need to wear espadrilles. Many a knee has been skinned on the bevelled rocks. Shrimping is a form of bullfighting in miniature: the shrimp dance around the net. How many lacerated feet and fractured coccyxes in order to catch a handful of tiny creatures that will be quickly shelled and eaten by the family before dinner like saltwater pistachios? To say nothing of the tar that gets stuck between your toes, brought courtesy of the constant Spanish oil slicks. In 1972 the Spanish were not the modern, the 'Almodovarised' people they are today; back then we thought of them chiefly as cleaning ladies with comedy accents, concierges with wispy moustaches, and vile polluters of our pristine coastline. My daughter, my darling, as soon as I get out of here I will take you to Cénitz. I must try not to think too much about you, nor about Priscilla, my love, who is probably worried to death. It's too painful. I would give my right arm for a Xanax .5mg. The walls are closing in. I'm starting to panic that I'll be given a custodial sentence, since the penal code allows for a sentence of up to one year in prison simply for using narcotics. I refused to call a lawyer because I was sure I would be released from custody in the morning. I naïvely assumed I was safe, when in fact I am simply a plaything in the hands of officials dehumanised by Taylorism – the cop who bangs you up is not the one who arrested you, and the judge who sentences you doesn't know the cop who banged you up, and if you protest your innocence you are only doing what every other defendant does, so it is the fourth official who nods sympathetically as he stamps your police record.

# 23

## RUE MAÎTRE-ALBERT

When my father was single again, he moved into a split-level apartment in the 5th arrondissement with exposed beams and a white, deep-pile carpet. My brother and I each had our own bedroom on the first floor, but we only stayed there about once a month. At the time, my father was thirty-five: eight years younger than I am as I write this. Who am I to judge my father's turbulent thirties from the dizzy heights of being fortysomething and in a prison cell? In my mind, my father changes completely after his divorce: the busy executive has nothing in common with the student obsessed with classical philosophy posing self-consciously in his wedding photographs. He runs an American headhunting agency (my father is one of the pioneers who imported 'headhunting' to France as a profession), he travels around the world four times a year, he's a jet-setter in a Ted Lapidus suit and tie, confident as perhaps only unhappy men can be. He decides to puff out his chest and join the capitalist rat race; he is resigned to being successful. Rich, handsome and single, he often had people round to his apartment for cocktails. That one word encapsulates my whole childhood; I feel as though I spent the whole of the 1970s at cocktail parties. On the coffee tables there were magazines full of naked women: *Absolu*, *Look*, *Lui* ('The Magazine for the Modern Man') between a couple of copies of *L'Expansion* or *Fortune*. My father was a businessman with a briefcase, an Aston Martin DB6 and Cuban cigars, none of which stopped him considering everything with a certain elegant disdain, an ironic detachment, a droll erudition, a pitiless sense of ridicule. Seneca and *Les Thibault* dozed on his bedside table beneath matchbooks from the Oriental in Bangkok, the Singapore Hilton or the Sheraton in Sydney. The fauna of the rue Maître-Albert were gay and insouciant; this was before the first oil crisis. This generation was living through the golden age of materialism; the world was less dangerous than it is today. It was a dream that lasted thirty years. On the marble console in the lobby were cards for various clubs: Le Privé, the Élysées-Matignon, Griffin's in Geneva, Regine's in New York, Castel, Diners Club International, Maxim's Business Club, Annabel's in London,

L'Apocalypse . . . The ashtrays were filled with coins from every country, next to executive toys (steel balls hanging on threads that swung back and forth making a clack-clack sound) or gadgets brought back from New York (the first Timex watch with a red liquid crystal display, the first electronic chess set, the first calculator from Texas Instruments, a plastic folding telephone or, much later, the first Sony Walkman). My father had a thing for gadgets; in my eyes he was a sort of James Bond: he looked like James Coburn in *Our Man Flint.* I remember my awe when he first got power windows in his Aston Martin, the first electric sunroof (in his subsequent car, a Peugeot 604), the first Radiocom 2000 carphone, the first Betamax video recorder. He also collected statues of the Buddha, and old clocks which chimed every quarter-hour. On Saturday nights dozens of friends would trip over his children as they went to fetch bottles of Pierre Cardin champagne from the kitchen. I remember a very tall girl called Rose de Ganay; there was also the lead actress from Éric Rohmer's *Claire's Knee*, Laurence de Monaghan (she constantly told my father she wanted to adopt me, and I was more than willing!); and a Belgian model called Chantal who preferred to be known as Kim. Let's see, who else . . .? The Bogdanoff twins; Jean-Luc

Brunel, an agent at Karin Models; Emmanuel de Mandat-Grancey, who recently stood in the municipal elections in the 6th arrondissement for a 'minor right-wing party'; Prince Jean Poniatowski (who ran *Vogue* magazine at the time); the bespoke tailor Michel Barnes; Bertrand Maingard of the hostess agency Top Étoile; Bob Benamou the gallery-owner; Robert Monteux, the owner of *Revenu français*; and the ex-wife of the emperor of Indonesia Dewi Sukarno – I remember listening to records from Champs Disques with her daughter Karina, who had bought up the whole record shop. My father's apartment attracted a mixture of fashion models who smoked menthol cigarettes and jolly chaps who played backgammon, some of whom had no name but were identified by sartorial details: 'the blond guy with the hat and the earring' was a guy who drove a Rolls because he had made a fortune through a series of gadget shops located opposite the major department stores; 'the old guy in the leather jacket' was a white-haired man who was invariably accompanied by young girls studying drama . . . These people did not realise they were disciples of a particular belief system. It is what to me seems most old-fashioned about them these days: their optimism. The grown-ups often talked about a certain 'JJSS' – which stood for Jean-Jacques Servan-Schreiber, I would later discover – who was the embodiment of progress, or about Jean Lecanuet, 'the French JFK'. They took flights with Pan Am – there were always sponge bags with the Pan Am logo in my father's bathroom. Even today, I can't stand people who mock Seventies haircuts, Renoma suits in brown tweed with wide lapels, ties with fat knots, ankle boots in kid leather and men in fur-lined jackets who smelled of 'Moustache' aftershave from Rochas; I always feel as though they are mocking my childhood. I would go round with a bowl of Apéricube cheese cubes. The girls wanted to listen to bossa nova. I would put on an LP my father had just brought back from New York: the soundtrack album to *Jonathan Livingstone Seagull* by Neil Diamond. It had nothing to do with bossa nova, but the models loved (they still love) that mawkish music, you can take that as a tip from me; or *Year of the Cat* by Al Stewart is a guaranteed success – you'll have them clapping their hands and shrieking 'Wow'. I was completely comfortable around these older goddesses; I so wished the pretty girls in my *sixième* class at the Lycée Montaigne could see me surrounded by fashion models. My father would shout because his friends were stubbing out their cigarettes on the carpet. He was constantly asking me to go into the kitchen to fetch more ashtrays. His guests had no respect for him; some of them did not even know whose house they were in. Here and there girls were being cornered by fake photographers; most of them did not even speak French. I often felt I wasn't wanted, I got in the way of grown-up conversations, the models would laugh whenever I came into the room, fluttering their hands to dispel the sickly smoke of the 'beedis' or their spliffs, the men would lower their voices or apologise for having said 'slut' or 'fuck': 'Do you think he heard me?' 'Shh, that's Jean-Michel's kid . . .' 'Oops, promise you won't tell Daddy what I said?' 'Your daddy is so crazy, Freddy!' and my father would eventually look at his watch and then utter the fatal question, 'Don't you think it's high time you were in bed?' This was one of the phrases I heard most often in my life. If I often lie awake at night, it may well be just out of sheer pig-headedness.

The boisterous atmosphere at my father's place, with its soundtrack of wailing by José Feliciano – the Puerto Rican Ray Charles – the shrill laughter of foreign women, the peaty smell of whisky mingled with the smoke from the log fire crackling in the fireplace, the noise of car horns from the windows open onto the street, the constant clamour, the bowls of cashew nuts, the overflowing ashtrays with sometimes an empty amphetamine 'diet pill' among the cigarette butts, these 'modern' parties were in stark contrast to the austerity of the weekdays spent with my mother, who listened to depressing songs by Barbara, Serge Reggiani or Georges Moustaki, and rigorously respected school hours, through the tedium of winter days, the steaming bowl of Ricoré in the mornings, our heavy schoolbags cutting into our delicate shoulders, the filthy canteen where we daily ingested celery *remoulade* and diced mixed vegetables, the gloomy face of Roger Gicquel reading the nightly news on the colour TV rented from Locatel after we'd had dinner in the kitchen – *escalopes* in cream sauce, spaghetti and a yoghurt dessert made by Chambourcy, and we had to go to bed early because the next day would be exactly the same. My own divorce probably followed the same pattern, as far as my daughter sees it: she lives with her Maman, who is always there, who is affectionate and responsible, and she spends every other weekend with a father who is evasive, a womaniser and irresponsible. Which does she find more fun? It's so easy to come off second best. Having to look after a child diminishes you in her eyes: you become ordinary. Children are ungrateful. If you want to attract someone's attention, you have to leave them.

# 24

## CASSETTES

On weekends at my father's place, I started recording cassettes. I would make compilations of my favourite songs so he could listen to them in the car on his way to the airport. It became my principal occupation: putting an LP on the record player, checking the sound levels so that the diodes didn't go too far into the red and the needle on the VU meter on the amplifier of the hi-fi system didn't get stuck all the way on the right. I recorded all my songs on BASF or Maxell Chrome cassettes; these days I still create playlists on his iPod. The amount of time I spent watching equaliser lights flickering, tape spooling in the cassette recorder, the woofers booming fit to wake the neighbours . . . It was as beautiful as *2001: A Space Odyssey*. I would segue the tracks, creating shifting progressions in the rhythm, varying the mood and the style, trying to startle him by putting Petula Clark's 'Don't Sleep in the Subway' between two slow numbers

('Could it be Magic?' by Barry Manilow and 'Oh Lori' by the Alessi Brothers). I would stock up on singles at Raoul Vidal's record shop on the place Saint-Germain-des-Prés. The pre-teen fashions a new family for himself through the singers he idolises, finds a tribe who will welcome him: the fans of The Who's *Tommy* at school or the Bob Marley groupies seemed closer to me than my own brother. Between 1975 and 1980 came my reggae period, then punk, then ska, then coldwave. Music is still my favourite time machine; it is the quickest way to brood over the past: I'm convinced that my collection of crackling singles contains within it all the history that my brain has divested me of. These days, whenever I listen to 'Don't Sleep in the Subway' and the glorious chorus comes in, as beautiful and astonishing as the Beach Boys' 'God Only Knows' (which perhaps inspired it), I plunge back through time, as Proust writes: 'Nothing but a moment of the past? Perhaps it was a great deal more; something which, common to both past and present, is much more essential than these two.' This something is the little boy who watched the spinning labels of the 45 rpm EPs – on which my mother had sometimes crossed out her signature 'Christine Beigbeder' and once again become 'Christine de Chasteigner'. The record player made my head spin: the A–Z of labels: Flèche, Parlophone, Odeon, Stax, Atlantic, CBS, RCA, Arista, Reprise, Columbia, Vogue, A&M Records . . . Music had become the only link between my parents; these cassettes I recorded continued to bring them together. I was utterly spellbound, I spent entire afternoons, almost, motionless in front of a vinyl disc turning, the way rave kids in the Nineties could stare at fractal videos until dawn in a car park or a hangar. Even today, when I play vinyl records in a nightclub I am fascinated by the sensuality of this perpetual motion which leads the point of the stylus towards the centre of the machine. The concentric grooves moving towards the middle of the record like little waves upon a black sea lapping on a plastic shore. The circles that coil around the central label like ripples from a stone tossed into the water (though the footage would need to be played in reverse, since the ripples move towards the point of impact).

I would change my mind, make preliminary cassettes, replacing 'Don't Sleep in the Subway' with 'Dream a Little Dream of Me' by the Mamas & the Papas – I have only just realised as I write this that this choice of group was not innocent. I would re-record over the same tape several times, changing the label using Sellotape and Tipp-Ex, and soon the case would be covered in a chalky crust and scribbled graffiti. The tip of my Biro would sink into the white plaster like the hands of actors in the cement outside Grauman's Chinese Theatre on Hollywood Boulevard. I sculpted my first manuscripts in sound. Every song erased the songs that had come before, just as, in our minds, each new memory tramples the one before.

# 25

# THE REVEALING CHILD

At the age of nine, my daughter is going through the same stage of musical taste as me. Just now, she is obsessed with *Hannah Montana* and *High School Musical*; I helped her stick up Disney Channel posters of Miley Cyrus and Zac Efron in her bedroom. 'Just Wanna be with You' is our favourite song; she for the music, me for the lyrics.

The human animal is an explorer; perhaps at a certain age he stops looking forward and begins to look back. If he has procreated, he has a guide to help him revisit his younger self.

Chloë's effect on me is like that of Herbert George Wells's *The Time Machine*. Watching my daughter takes me back to my childhood. Everything Chloë sees, I see again, everything she discovers, I rediscover. Every time I take her to the Botanic Gardens, I return to paradise lost, I find again my footprints between the Enchanted River and the Ice Maze (I don't think the other attractions existed back in my day). The way she has of losing her fleece jacket, her Tamagotchi, the way she drops her sweaters in her wake remind me of how I used to leave my belongings lying around: my coat, my denim jacket, my marbles scattered like the pebbles Tom Thumb left in the Luxembourg forest. The Punch and Judy show hasn't changed: it's as lame as it was when I was little. Chloë's games are my DeLorean (the car from *Back to the Future*). Her colouring books and stickers, the mysterious sketch pads where you only have to run a pencil over the page and a drawing magically appears . . . even to me it seems miraculous, like the numbered dots you have to join up for something or someone to appear. The words of this book inspire the same feeling: 'Join the dots in order and you'll magically see . . . your forgotten childhood.' When Chloë is excited to find the charm hidden in the Pithiviers cake at Christmas, or proud of performing a magic trick though everyone can see how it was done, or histrionically happy every morning as she opens another cardboard window on her advent calendar, or disgusted to discover she's got head lice, or eager to drive past the Eiffel Tower with its twinkling lights, I know that I was once like that, even if my memory of it is vague – the lights on the Eiffel Tower did not twinkle in the 1970s, but in my mind that just made it all the more impressive, like a huge metal brontosaurus. The world is very different, and yet the phases are still the same. For example, despite the existence of the internet, of DVDs and three hundred television channels, Christmas has still not been overwhelmed by the deluge of entreaties. Something of the mystery remains. An appointment with wonder; a combination of the birth of Christ and Santa Claus coming down the chimney. I should point out one major difference between my daughter and me: she believed in Santa Claus, whereas I have no memory of ever playing along with that game. I was surprised that she cried so much when she finally found out, at the age of six, that her parents had been lying to her. She felt swindled, disappointed, disgusted.

'You did the same thing to me with the Tooth Fairy. Why do you have to lie to me all the time?'

I felt guilty about having duped Chloë. Who can you trust if your own parents tell you fibs? Good question, and one which will come up again later in this puzzle.

Thanks to her mother's genes, my daughter is a thousand times more beautiful than I was at her age. What she gets from me: her chin, her thinness, her buck teeth (she will have to wear braces like her father; if I were her, I'd sue me). Chloë does not laugh when you tickle her on the soles of her feet or under her arms. The only way to tickle her is by playing *the little bug that climbs and climbs.* My hand starts its journey at her bellybutton, the ticklish fingers climbing towards her neck, and as it comes closer she wriggles, clamps her chin to her chest, she squirms and thrashes, but not too hard because she craves and dreads what is coming next, she wants this torture she does not want, and the 'little bug' that is my fingers climbs and climbs up her swan-like neck and will soon reach her chin . . . and at this point she can stand it no longer and her peal of laughter is a cure-all to me; I should record it so that I can play it on nights when I am depressed. If I had to define the joy of life, the bliss of simply existing, it would be that peal of laughter, my apotheosis, my blessed reward, like a balm sent from heaven.

The first time she tasted Chamonix orange cookies, I recognised the sensation. I know she eats very little, that she never seems hungry. I used to be like her (how things change!). Though I was never anorexic, I ate very little: I am careful not to tell her that at her age if I was forced to clear my plate, I would roll the food into a ball in my cheek like a squirrel and then go and spit it out in 'the smallest room', as my grandmother called it. It is strange to watch someone follow in your footsteps. I am close to you because I preceded you there, and there, and there too; all these things you think you are the first person in the world to imagine, to feel, are things that I imagined, that I felt, when I was your age. The swings, where my daughter likes to stand up and bend her knees to fly higher, are the same swings where I skinned my knees; like her I remember merry-go-rounds that made me queasy, my fingers sticky with candy floss, my abiding hatred of grated carrots, the sweets in big jars in the kiosks at Luco: chewy toffees, liquorice sticks that tasted like trees, chewing gum that came in tubes, shells, bracelets of multi-coloured sweets. And going to the cinema in the afternoon . . . Another memory has come back, like a spatiotemporal boomerang. In the Aston Martin, the eight-track stereo blasting out 'I'm Looking Through You' by the Beatles: 'I'm looking through you/Where did you go?/I thought I knew you/What did I know?' After the divorce, my father would take my brother and me to lunch at the fashionable new restaurant, Hippopotamus, before going to the movies on Sunday afternoons without having to worry about starting times. Back then, on the Grands Boulevards, they had 'non-stop cinema'. You could go in the middle of the film, embarrassed at forcing everyone in the row to get up, then try to work out what was happening on the screen. Often, it was something to do with cowboys, the moment when the hero gets an arrow in his shoulder which has to be ripped out and the wound cauterised with a red-hot brand – though not before his best mate gives him a swig of whiskey as anaesthetic and a piece of wood to bite down on. Then there were the movies with dinosaurs (*The Land that Time Forgot*) or with English submarines being attacked by German torpedoes. Or *Ben-Hur* at the Kinopanorama on the avenue de la Motte-Picquet (with an intermission in the middle). Since Papa had never really known how to talk to us, he used to take us to see the Francis Lopez operettas at the Théâtre de Châtelet (I remember *Gypsy* with José Todaro), or to the circus at Cirque Amar (I thought it was all one word, 'Cirqueamar', like 'Miramar'), before my brother and I became fervent movie buffs: there was the Marx Brothers era at the Cinéma Mac Mahon, the Jacques Tati era at the Champo, the Mel Brooks era – Papa was as much a fan as we were

(*Blazing Saddles*, *Silent Movie*, *The Producers* and *Young Frankenstein*, which scared me half to death), the Inspector Clouseau era, there were all the Sensurround movies where the seats shook – *Earthquake*, *Avalanche*, *The Battle of Midway* . . . When the house lights came on we would stay in the cinema and wait for the film we'd just seen the end of to start up again. Usually there were cartoons (Tom and Jerry, Bugs Bunny or Road Runner and Wile E. Coyote), followed by advertisements for the Aéroport de Paris which used the Bee Gees' 'I Started a Joke' or Nilsson's 'Without You' as a soundtrack, and ads for things that these days don't exist (Cadbury's Wafers, Supercarambar, Topset, Picorette, or Fruité with the little jingle that went, 'We're not the sort of people to get caught up in a hustle/ Fruité is a drink that has much more muscle') or are considered old-fashioned (Chocoletti, Ovomaltine, the Canada Dry ads in which Eliot Ness is forced to let Al Capone go with the slogan 'It looks like alcohol, it tastes like alcohol, but it's not alcohol' . . .) Usherettes would walk up and down the aisles selling sweets from wicker baskets that hung from their necks. My father would pass a five-franc bill with the portrait of Victor Hugo from hand to hand until it reached the woman, who would send back down the row a Mint'ho for him and two Gervais ice-cream bars for us (vanilla for me, chocolate for Charles). Papa often told the same jokes – 'That's my opinion and I agree with me,' for example. Or he'd call us 'sons of idiots', which made us laugh. Then the lights would go down and we would finally get to see the beginning of the movie, having already seen the end. For example, having already seen the chariot race where Ben-Hur fights to the death with the evil Messala, we found out that they were best friends at the start. You may have noticed that the structure of this book is highly influenced by 'non-stop cinema': I put the end at the beginning, and I'm hoping that it will end with a beginning (me being released?).

On the subject of my father's choice of films, I've just remembered something traumatic: one day Papa took us to see *Papillon* when we were much too young to see a film about Devil's Island. Charles and I took it in turns to cry, shielding our eyes with our scarves. We stuck our fingers in our ears and hummed so as not to hear the prisoners screaming. We kept going to the toilet so as not to see the blood, the torture, the escape attempts that were viciously punished, Dustin Hoffman in a pit feeding on woodlice . . . I've never been able to watch the film again, not even now, thirty years later. I have to stop thinking about it now, otherwise, banged up in this cell, I'll start thinking I'm Steve McQueen eating cockroaches and licking dried vomit off the floor. Curiously (though is it really surprising?), my mind seems to conjure a lot of memories related to imprisonment: the visit to Alcatraz, the screening of *Papillon* . . .

# 26

## A SCIENTIFIC DIGRESSION

To pass the time, I eavesdrop on my guards' conversations. One of them is showing the other an article in the Science section of *Le Monde*: '"Forgotten" Memories can be Rekindled by Mild Electrical Stimulation to the Brain'. Apparently a man being treated for obesity using Deep Brain Stimulation relived a scene that had taken place thirty years earlier. It happened in Canada: the patient thought he was in a park with friends. Among the people there he recognised his girlfriend of the time. He could see them walk and talk, though he could not quite make out what they were saying. He viewed the scene in colour as an observer, and therefore did not see himself. I have to get to the Western Hospital in Toronto to have my hypothalamus stimulated. But before I do that, I'll have to eat a lot to become obese. I'm starving to death here and losing my marbles.

Since my daughter is capable of restoring my

memories, I deduce that a child can activate an intracranial electrode. Watching her probably sets off electrical discharges in my brain. One possible definition of love: an electroshock that can rekindle memory.

# 27

# THE TRIP ACROSS PARIS

At 2 p.m., I am told the public prosecutor has ordered that I be transferred to the Hôtel Dieu so I can pee in a test tube. This is a terrible disappointment: the inspector who interviewed me this morning told me I would be released after a night in the cells; clearly this is not going to happen. Four officers put me in handcuffs and bundle me into a prison van that takes me across Paris. I pull my jacket over my head in case the paparazzi are following us. The trip to the hospital for a urine analysis is like a breath of fresh air. I have finally been let out of that revolting little cell in which I spent the night suffocating . . . When we arrive at the Hôtel Dieu my illusions are shattered. The duty doctor is at lunch. I wait with a variety of other suspects: a junky going through withdrawal, face grey, sweating, frantically scratching his arm; a dealer who constantly proclaims his innocence; a con man who gives him a high-five as soon as his cuffs are removed: they know each other, they've already shared a cell. Eventually, the doctor deigns to come back from lunch and a police officer hands me a white plastic cup.

'OK, um, you need to urinate into this.'

He points to the toilets. The problem is, I feel no urge to piss: I've been pissing all morning. As soon as I realised that the only possible distraction was going to the toilet, I made the most of it. The warders are obliged to open the cell and lead you down the corridor, which means you get to stretch your legs. Right now I am incapable of producing so much as a droplet for the forces of law and order, so I re-emerge from the toilet clutching my empty plastic cup. I find myself face to face with fifteen uniformed officers, all of them dismayed by this situation: one of France's most infamous authors, arrested for snorting a little gutter glitter, is unable to piss in their cup. It's not exactly something you'd want to write home about. I ask for some water, drink three glasses, and go back and sit with my new drug-dealer mates. The guy who's just told the police that he is absolutely not a dealer says to me: 'What the fuck are you doing here? I've seen you somewhere before. You're on TV, aren't you?'

I am surprised to discover that my vocal cords still work.

'Drug use in a public place.'

'Weed?'

'Coke.'

'Ha ha ha! You're off your fucking head, mate! Did you snort it off your hand, or off a wheelie bin?'

'Off the bonnet of a car.'

'Maximum respect! You're my fucking hero!' (He lowers his voice.) 'If you need any gear, I can hook you up. Here, this is my number.'

'Er . . . the thing is . . .'

'Swear down, it's the best in the 18th arrondissement. Venezuelan fishscale. Pure and all natural.'

'You're telling me dealers have started a line of organic class As?'

'Absofuckinglutely – guaranteed no genetically modified crops!'

We laugh about this. The smack addict going cold turkey attempts a smile. The glorious fraternisation of junkies on remand. Prison really is a great way of meeting people. Finally, my bladder wakes up. I go back to the toilet, escorted by a troop of officers worthy of a head of state. I emerge with my beakerful of warm yellow liquid. Then the duty doctor does a brief examination; I remember the mythical phrase 'Your blood pressure is abnormally high, but that's perfectly normal given what you've been through.' I cross Paris again in the back of a police van, handcuffed, bouncing around, my wrists aching. I try to joke with the guards: 'You can drop me off here, I just spotted a lovely bonnet on a Bentley!' Some of them ask for autographs, others tell me they arrested the journalist Jean-Pierre Elkabbach for driving in a bus lane, and he was a lot less compliant than me (he threatened to call the Élysée Palace!). It is 5 p.m. when the officers once again close the door on my cell in the 8th arrondissement police station. The good news: the Poet is still there, and he's finally sobered up. His breath still reeks of booze since he didn't get to brush his teeth last night, a new fresh scent we might call 'vodkaesque'. He doesn't remember anything: not his arrest, not our pitiful attempt to escape, not the hellish night spent locked in this subterranean dungeon. He tells me the police have searched his apartment with junkie sniffer-dogs. They didn't find anything, but the poor dogs suffering from withdrawal kept sniffing the coffee table on the spot where he usually cuts his gear. Homeopathy gave us water memory; now we have furniture memory. The Poet was carrying three grams when he was arrested, not having thought to ditch the coke while we were being chased. He's afraid they suspect him of intent to supply. If so, he risks being banged up for years . . . Still, he seems less worried than I am. It's like water off a duck's back to him. His pessimism is like an armour: he is so ready to believe the worst that he is never surprised. I, on the other hand, am furious. We don't deserve to be treated like this. I've gone for almost twenty-four hours with no sleep. My hair is greasy, my armpits stink, I disgust myself. For indulging in illicit substances, two French writers have been arrested and held in separate cells with no natural light, miniature cages with blinding fluorescent lights in which it is impossible to tell day from night, where it is impossible to sleep for the screams, the insults and the cramped conditions, cut off from the world, entitled to only one phone call which we are not allowed to make ourselves: in the end it was a female cop who called the mother of my child to tell her I was being held at Sarij 8 and that I would therefore not be available to pick Chloë up from school today. I'd read an article on the prison conditions of student protesters in Tehran: they're exactly the same as those in the 8th arrondissement of Paris. The only difference is that in Tehran they are whipped with electric cables. When I say this, the Poet says mockingly, 'Yeah, some people have all the luck.'

His warped humour calms me, and I finally smile.

'Yes, oh yesss! Whip us, whip us pleaaaase!'

'We are all Iranian students!'

'We are all Bulgarian nurses – remember the Bulgarian nurses in Libya?'

'We demand Cécilia Sarkozy, she got the Bulgarian nurses released!'

'No, fuck Cécilia, we want Carla Bruni!'

'WE WANT CÉ-CI-LIA!'

'WE WANT CAR-LA! CAR-LA! CAR-LA!'

The commissioner shows up.

'Are we having fun here?'

'Commissioner, I'm prepared to confess to any crime, just like the suspects in the Outreau trial. Yes, I raped those children. Yes, I'm the Japanese guy who murdered and cannibalised a Dutch woman. Yes, yes, yes, whatever you want. If I sign a confession can I get out of here?'

The commissioner is used to such tactics; he can tell that behind the jokes I'm shitting bricks.

'Take it easy. When the public prosecutor gets the results of your urine analysis, he'll let you out. You've got no previous.'

'Twenty-four hours in custody for some pathetic partying? I tell you, French society has gone fucking mad!'

'That's our orders these days. Since we can't stop drug trafficking, we take it out on the users.

It's just like prostitution: we arrest the johns. If there's no customers, there's no problem.'

'That's completely insane . . .'

'It's the same thing with paedophiles. Since we can't stop perverts abusing children, we arrest people for downloading paedophile videos from the internet.'

'But you must see that it's completely unjust. Some guy jerks off watching a video, another guys snorts a line of blow, a third guy fucks some Albanian whore, all that might be heinous, I grant you, but it's LESS HEINOUS than the guy who recorded the video, the guy who imported a ton of coke, and the pimp who beats up the prostitute from Tirana.'

'What do you expect? If there's no demand, there's no supply.'

'You're talking like an economist! Arresting the depraved is a slippery slope that leads to dictatorship. You don't seem to realise it, but you're supporting a return to a moral order that's completely fascist.'

'As far as the French health system is concerned, you're collateral damage . . . We try to safeguard the health of our citizens, because the cost to society is enormous. You do know that after you turn forty, every line of coke you do is a potential heart attack?'

'Gee, thanks, I've been struggling with the French health police since the early hours of this morning!'

The Poet begins to recite a text: 'A Government founded upon the principle of Benevolence towards the people – after the analogy of a *father* to his children, and therefore called a *paternal government* – would be one in which the Subjects would be regarded as children or minors unable to distinguish what is beneficial or injurious to them. These subjects would be thus compelled to act in a merely passive way; and they would be trained to expect solely from the Judgment of the Sovereign and just as he might will it, merely out of his goodness, all that ought to make them happy. Such a Government would be the greatest conceivable *Despotism*.'

'Who wrote that?'

'Kant, from *On the Old Saw: That May be Right in Theory* . . ., published in 1793.'

'Oscar Wilde said the same thing more succinctly: "You can't make people good by Act of Parliament."'

A little later another officer brought us another plastic tray of microwaved stewed beef and carrots. The menu here is the same every day. This must mean it is dinner time. It is probably dark outside. I refuse to touch this slop, I start a hunger strike. At this point, I'm still sure that I'll be out in time to have dinner at Brasserie Lipp. I haven't yet met Jean-Claude Marin.

I cannot here give full vent to the high regard in which I hold J-C. Jean-Claude Marin is the Procureur de Paris – the public prosecutor: you have to be really careful when you write stuff about him, which is probably why no one ever talks about Jean-Claude Marin. That morning, 29 January 2008, Jean-Claude Marin arrived in his office. He hung his coat on a peg, sat down and picked up my file. Jean-Claude Marin had asked that all cases involving celebrities should be referred to him. Physically, Jean-Claude Marin looks like Alban Ceray (the porn star), but his life is a lot less entertaining. Jean-Claude Marin was appointed Procureur de Paris by Jacques Chirac. Since that time, Jean-Claude Marin has requested additional information, launched preliminary investigations, appealed against judgements, filed away cold cases; the humdrum life of the average public prosecutor is not exactly thrilling. And yet it should be said that Jean-Claude Marin can ruin the life of any citizen living in the French capital. Jean-Claude Marin can send a team of cops round to my house, or to my publisher Grasset, whenever he feels like it. In photographs, Jean-Claude Marin wears a godawful tie and a striped shirt so that no one will realise how powerful he is (this is JCM's camouflage). On 29 January 2008, for example, Jean-Claude Marin receives my urine analysis confirming what everybody already knew (*Oh là là*, I took drugs with a mate, the whole French state is threatened!) and decides to let me rot in prison for another night. The police argue the toss with Jean-Claude Marin. They tell Jean-Claude Marin that I'm only a user, that I have admitted the charges and that there is no need to extend police custody. But Jean-Claude Marin thinks that my novel *£9.99* is an apologia for cocaine use. Which proves he hasn't read it – because of his addiction, Octave, the hero of the book, loses his wife and his job then takes an overdose and goes into rehab, before ending up in prison as an accessory to murder. It also proves that Jean-Claude Marin makes no distinction between fiction and reality, between character and author. It's not his fault: J-C is not a man of letters, he is a man of law. And so, that terrible afternoon, Jean-Claude Marin decided to give a firm lesson in claustrophobia to a 'people' who hasn't slept a wink all night. The first night punished Frédéric, we must now punish Octave.

Jean-Claude Marin seems to think he's my father. Get thee behind me, stranger! I barely tolerate your presence in this book, interloper! But you are not one of my family. For your information, Jean-Claude Marin, you are a prisoner serving a life sentence in this book. I have power too: in Chapter 27, I am permanently remanding you in custody. So you wanted to come over all Jean-Claude? Well, I will offer you a little more publicity. For generations to come, the words Jean, Claude and Marin will not be a long-forgotten first name and surname but a symbol of the Blind Biopolitics of Paternalistic Prohibition. If you will allow me, my little Jean-Claude, common courtesy demands that I immortalise you for centuries to come, since Ronsard did not dedicate an ode to your ancestors. What do you say? Thank you Freddy, Count of Monte-Cristo!

# 28

# BROTHER OF THE ABOVE-NAMED

What if Freud were wrong? What if the most important thing was not father and mother, but brother? It seems to me that all my actions, for as long as I can remember, have been dictated by my older brother. All I have done is imitate him, rebel against him, compare myself to him, create myself in relation to him. We are separated by a year and a half; it was not enough: we were sham twins. The problem is that Charles is unbeatable, he is the perfect man. He thereby left me only one option: to be the imperfect man.

What is a younger brother? A friend? An enemy? An ersatz son? A plagiarist? A slave? A rival? An interloper? A younger version of oneself? It is your own blood that infuriates you, it is recognising yourself in another. A new You. Jean-Bertrand Pontalis wrote a clear-sighted piece about siblings entitled 'Brother of the Above-Named'. This probably best defines my identity: I was the brother of the above-named. Subconsciously, I have probably done everything in my power to ensure that wherever he goes, when my brother introduces himself to someone, they ask whether he is related to me. In the beginning there was Charles, whose eyes were so much bluer; Charles, whose teeth were immaculately white. I was the leukaemic younger brother, the puny little runt, the scrawny kid with a profile like a crescent moon, a concave face.

It is not easy being the elder, being expected to set an example. The one who makes all the mistakes, the dethroned king, the preliminary sketch for the second child, a substitute father? As Cain with Abel, my brother spent his childhood trying to kill me. Once, he almost succeeded in Pau while running after me with a screwdriver in the playroom in the basement of the Villa Navarre. My cousin Geraldine saved me by interposing herself. On another occasion he threw pétanque boules at my head while I was dancing to avoid these steel and chrome projectiles. My cousin Édouard, who is a couple of years younger, was hugely impressed by our violent outbursts. These days, Édouard Beigbeder does humanitarian aid work for UNICEF; he has been to

Rwanda, to Bosnia, to Ossetia, to Sri Lanka in the wake of the tsunami; I think he has seen more horrors than most of the people I know. Yet still he remembers my shrieks of terror when Charles used to chase me. My older brother also tried to drown me, holding my head underwater in every pool and in every sea in which we swam; it is thanks to him that I became an expert at holding my breath – even today I can easily stay underwater for two minutes. Another technique consisted of smothering me with a pillow, kneeling on my shoulders to pin me down. I never held any of this against him because I provoked him constantly, destroying everything he built, whether a Lego house, a sandcastle or a model aeroplane. My father also had an elder brother who was domineering, quick-tempered and constantly humiliated him (Gérald Beigbeder); he has cordially detested him his whole life. The hatred of an elder for a younger sibling is natural (the new child has stolen what was rightfully his), but it is not always reciprocated. From an early age I adopted a sardonic, Gandhi-like approach. I continually thumbed my nose at my brother's authority. The only difference between my strategy and that of the Mahatma was that I would sometimes launch a surprise attack, planting my bony knee in his thigh and yelling 'Dead-leg!' – a non-non-violent tactic which, to my knowledge, the founder of modern India never employed. These dead legs would later lead to greenish yellow bruises on my brother's legs. In this light, his attempted fratricide can therefore be considered self-defence. All in all, we were two ordinary brothers with bruises by way of medals.

Winding my brother up was my way of breaking the family fate. Charles and I did not want to be like the previous generation: my father had fallen out with his brother; they sued each other over their inheritance and could not agree about the running of the health spas in Béarn. My constant taunting was my twisted way of saying 'I love you, Charles'. There you go, I've said it, I'll never say it again, once in a lifetime is enough. Pontalis suggests that love, hatred or friendship can exist between brothers, and sometimes a mixture of all three. On a scale of fraternal feeling running from homosexual incest to fratricide, I'd say we were bang in the middle, oscillating between mutual fascination and feigned indifference. Very early I lost the fight and realised that everything was settled: he would have an orderly life, while mine would be chaotic. But we were united in adversity: if anyone attacked either of us, the other was prepared to die to defend him.

Charles was domineering but protective. We were united by our nasty, cruel, mischievous sense of humour, our constant jibes, and I couldn't help but laugh when he called me a 'lackey' and ordered me to bring 'the victuals' to the table . . . Or in a restaurant when he grilled the head waiter: 'Is your Camembert ripe?' And when the man said, 'I think so,' Charles would snap, 'You think so? Would you be so good as to go and check.' Ah, to my dying day that 'Would you be so good . . .' will make me laugh till I cry.

I grew up under the yoke of this splendid dictator, but, thank God, his totalitarianism was tempered by self-mockery. He was born on the same day as Adolf Hitler, as I reminded him all too often. It was, I claimed, proof that astrology is an exact science. My mother constantly had to intervene. When Chloë complains about being an only child, I tell her: 'You don't know how lucky you are!' That's how it is in all families, I don't hold it against my brother. I was the younger, he had to vanquish me, to crush the usurper, the superfluous child, in order to remain the great Charles, and I had to resist in order to impose my difference, my independence, in order to become Frédéric. In this way, Charles made his little brother stronger.

* * *

How can you kill the father when he's not at home? All that remained was the brother. We each applied Oedipal theory in our own way.

The highs and lows of our mother's love life caused collateral damage: riches from zero to age six, poverty from six to eight, luxury from eight to fourteen, lean times from age fourteen to eighteen. In her little white Fiat 127, my mother would cart us from vast apartments to tiny hovels. Let no one accuse my mother of being mercenary: it was because she was a romantic that, on two separate occasions, she did not hesitate to leave opulent homes to go and live with her sons in straitened circumstances, taking on the poorly paid translation of moronic Harlequin romances in order to pay the rent. One day we each had our own bedroom, and the next we would be back in bunk beds. We were never destitute: it was only ever jumpers with patches on the elbows. At the age of seventeen, on the rue Coëtlogon, my brother and I shared a bedroom with blue wallpaper. Sometimes we would even entertain girls in our single beds; sometimes Charles would make love quietly, one hand over his girlfriend's mouth, while I pretended to be asleep. At night when Charles asked me to stop coughing and wanking, I would tell him to stop grinding his teeth and snoring. When he was revising maths, I would crank up Blue Oyster Cult. Cohabiting is no easy thing. We both got the fuck out of there as soon as we were old enough, and grew apart afterwards. He was probably relieved; I never got over it.

I don't know whether we grew apart because we were different, or vice versa: perhaps I deliberately tried to be different because life would separate us, and because being his antithesis was my only hope of getting through this new divorce. We each had our lives to live, and I knew we could not live them together. It was when we split up that I realised how fond I was of my fake twin. I have spent my whole life, since he left home, seeking out a substitute big brother. Older friends who would tell me where to go, what to do (what Americans call a 'role model'). From an early age I was accustomed to following someone headstrong enough for two.

Don't get me wrong: Charles gives meaning to my life. I create myself in opposition to him. It may be stupid, but at the age of ten, being different was the only way I could think to define myself. Being yin to his yang, tails to his heads, his shadow self, his warped reflection, his backseat driver, his inverted double (*Doppelgänger* in German), the flipside of his portrait, his Shadow Cabinet, his alter ego (the one who alters his ego), his Mister Hyde. He likes to create? I like to criticise. He's good at maths? I'll work hard in French. He likes board games? I'll play pinball with my mates. He's a practising Catholic? I'll be a contemptuous heathen. I liked aniseed and liquorice BECAUSE he didn't like them. To my brother's board games, I preferred solo arcade games where I could insert a two-franc piece and frantically fire at anything that moved: brick walls, aliens in Space Invaders, meteors in Asteroids, and aliens and meteors in Defender . . . From an early age, everything was decided: at nine, Charles read *Picsou* magazine and collected model trains; today he juggles colossal investments in electricity and claims he wants to rival the SNCF. People don't change, childhood forever defines us, because society has infantilised us for life. At the same age, I read *Pif Gadget* (a communist rag). I played Jokari in the garden at Patrakénéa, wildly lashing at the ball attached to a piece of elastic that kept coming back to bug me. Jokari is probably the most pathetic game in the whole world: a sort of cross between *pelote* and a boomerang – like literature, it is the one sport where you can be sure you WILL

NEVER WIN. Without Charles, I no longer know who I am, I'm lost. The man is my anchor though he does not know it – he thinks I don't give a shit about him. To this day, he has been my point of reference. You think this kind of playacting stops when you're an adult? You must be joking: he's been married for twelve years; I've been divorced twice. He's a member of MEDEF, the largest employers' union in France; I was an adviser to the French Communist Party. He gets the Légion d'honneur, I get banged up. It's a short step from the Élysée Palace to the gaol. One brother grows up to earn a fortune and have a medal pinned on him, while the other, who is almost identical, who grew up alongside him, was raised by the same mother, finds himself bare-arse naked, surrounded by cops, shivering on a plank of wood. I hope that this shameless chapter does not offend him. In a book he published last year, he recounted a different version: 'There was never any competition between us'; obviously not, since he was the victor.

Is my monogamous brother happier than I am? I have to confess that decency and faith seem to have brought him greater happiness than hedonism and materialism have brought me; from the beginning, he has been the true radical, the real headcase, the genuine rebel of the family, though I did not realise it, whereas my wild, drug-fuelled parties, my life as an overgrown teenager, is merely meek subservience to prevailing trends. The capitalist injunction (everything that is pleasurable is obligatory) is as stupid as Christian guilt (everything that is pleasurable is forbidden). I party to forget, incapable of growing up, whereas he has built his life around a solid marriage, children who love him, a religion that is eternal, a house with a beautiful garden. I revel in the night, give myself airs, when in fact of the two of us, I am the more bourgeois. In fleeing my family, I did not realise that I was succumbing to a far greater alienation: the submission to an amnesiac individualism. Stripped of family ties, we are merely interchangeable numbers, like Facebook 'friends', jobseekers at the dole office or prisoners in the Dépôt du Palais de Justice.

I lost my father at the age of seven and my brother at the age of eighteen. And yet they are still the two men in my life.

# 29

# COULD TRY HARDER

When I was young, no one ever wore a seatbelt. Everyone smoked everywhere. They necked booze while they were driving. Weaved around on mopeds wearing no helmet. I remember the Formula 1 driver Jacques Laffite driving my father's Aston Martin at 270 kph in order to inaugurate the new Biarritz–San Sebastián motorway. People fucked without condoms. You were allowed to stare at a woman, go up to her, try to seduce her, maybe even brush up against her, without being thought of as a criminal. The main difference between my parents and me is that throughout their youth freedoms increased, whereas during mine, year on year, they were curtailed.

It is unarguable that in the writer, the Pursuit of Fleeting Pleasure reduces life expectancy. Jacques Vaché died aged twenty-three of an opium overdose, Jean de Tinan aged twenty-four of rheumatism aggravated by drinking adulterated alcohol, Georg

Trakl aged twenty-seven of a cocaine overdose, Hervé Guibert aged thirty-six of AIDS, Roger Nimier aged thirty-six of an accident while driving an Aston Martin, Boris Vian aged thirty-nine of the effects of too much wild living on a delicate heart, Guillaume Dustan at forty of a drug overdose, Guy de Maupassant at forty-three of syphilis, Scott Fitzgerald at forty-four of alcoholism, Charles Baudelaire at forty-six of syphilis, Alfred de Musset at forty-six of alcoholism, Albert Camus at forty-six in a car accident as a passenger in a Facel Vega, Jack Kerouac at forty-seven of cirrhosis, Malcolm Lowry at forty-seven of an overdose of sleeping pills, Frédéric Berthet at forty-nine of alcoholism, Jean Lorrain at fifty of peritonitis resulting from drinking ether, Hans Fallada at fifty-three of a morphine overdose, Paul-Jean Toulet at fifty-three of an overdose of laudanum . . . Since I lack the talent of my literary masters, Lord, may I also hope to be spared their brief lifespan? Since having a child, I have given up my dreams of dying young.

Towards 7 p.m., the officer who had interrogated me came back to my kennel, his face pale, to say: 'It's incredible, I've never seen the like of it. You're being transferred to the Dépôt. I don't get it.'

He sighs, though not as much as I do. In the past twenty-four hours I have oscillated between disappointment and false hope. My suffering comes not simply from being incarcerated but from hopes constantly thwarted. I think about my cat, locked in my apartment, probably starving to death. In this absurd world I almost find myself having to console the cop who is about to go home to bed.

'You'll be transferred in a police van to the Île de la Cité, where you'll spend another night in the cells. The public prosecutor will see you tomorrow. I'm sorry, but I'm going to have to cuff you again.'

'But what does all this mean? Are we going to be given a custodial sentence?'

'I've no idea. The case file we were sent was completely empty. It's not standard procedure to extend custody in a simple case of possession, but what can I tell you? . . . Maybe the fact you snorted it off the bonnet of a car pissed him off. Or maybe he just wants to make an example, to stick it to someone famous.'

The law holds that a drug user can be sentenced to up to one year in prison for smoking a spliff, ripping a rail, popping a pill, shooting up. But the Poet is stunned; he is starting to worry about being charged with something worse. (Beigbeder's dealer? That would be pretty serious . . .) He starts apologising.

'This is all my fucking fault. Jesus, I'm so sorry.'

'Shut up. There's nothing you can do now.'

'I've finally given you the one thing your destiny lacked: a fall from grace. "Woe betide those whom woe has spared . . ."'

'Is that one of your lines?'

'Yeah.'

'Can I put it in my novel?'

'OK.'

Done and done.

I can no longer work out what causes me more pain: the exhaustion, the anger, the claustrophobia, the discomfort, the shame and now the blind panic. Cudgel blows raining down on my head, on this face like a terrified bearded gargoyle with rancid breath and mad, bulging eyes ringed with dark circles. The night that is just beginning will be the longest of my entire life. I thought the nightmare was over; it is only beginning. From the moment the heavy metal door clangs shut on the knot in my stomach, I am nothing but a shadow, a wild-eyed slave, a zombie who allows himself to be led from A to B, hands cuffed behind his back, pale, compliant, mute, dazed. I solemnly declare that on that night, people to whom I had never done any harm decided to revoke my humanity, and they succeeded. They led a child into the white police van; they drove a lamb to the slaughter.

# 30

# FORCE-FED CHILDREN

Divorce multiplies everything: suddenly you have two apartments, two Christmases, two bedrooms, a double life. And yet this divorce slashed me in half; I felt somehow amputated: I became a half-baked, half-hearted half-wit, I became half a man. My parents' separation relegated them to their different worlds: Papa to the eccentric bourgeoisie, Maman to the impoverished aristocracy. The credit sequence of *The Persuaders*, a series first broadcast on French TV as *Amicalement vôtre* in 1972, seemed to me to sum up my parents. It's a split-screen job – on the right side of the screen, Lord Brett Sinclair, an English aristocrat, sophisticated, snobbish, wearing a cravat (my mother, as played by Roger Moore); on the left, Danny Wilde, the Yankee upstart, vulgar, laid-back, funny (my father, as played by Tony Curtis). My father's apartment was more ostentatious: there was a man who worked as cook-cum-chauffeur, a steady stream of girlfriends, an exuberant loneliness that was lonely just the same. At my mother's we felt more cramped; it was less spacious but much warmer because this was real life, everyday life, with a loving mother rather than a manservant. Divorce taught me to compartmentalise. To lead a double life, to hone the gifts of ubiquity and duplicity. Not to talk about Papa when I was at Maman's, or about Maman when I was with Papa. Above all, never to compare them. The television set at my mother's was a rental, whereas my father owned his. Papa would drop us off outside 22, rue Monsieur-le-Prince so as not to run into Maman. We had to take the stairs four at a time, open the door, rush into the living room, throw open the window overlooking the street and wave to let Papa know we had got in safely. I learned to be as happy in a tiny flat hardly fifty metres square as in a three-storey apartment five times as big. To go on acting as though everything was normal since, as Maman always put it, we were 'lucky, when you think about the poor little children in Ethiopia'. Our bellies were bloated not by malnutrition but by chocolate éclairs. Our eyes were not crawling with flies but framed by glasses. When I prayed for the little Ethiopian children at Mass at the Lycée Bossuet, I mostly prayed not to be like them.

* * *

I make no moral judgement about my parents' divorce, given that I inflicted the same thing on my own child. But let us stop denying that this new way of living moulds a child's character. These days it is the norm to have two houses, four parents (minimum), to love people who no longer love each other, to be constantly worried people will break up, to have to console one's parents, to listen to two different versions of every event like a judge at a trial.

The children of parents who divorced in 1972 were left utterly exposed to the winds of modern hedonism: the first Liberation (1945) paved the way for the cult of wealth; the second (1968) bred greedy, insatiable sensualists. As a reaction, the children of these doubly liberated adults instinctively developed a fear of freedom. Consequently, the children of parents who divorced in the 1970s are all:

- workaholics who pretend to be laid-back
- squares who pretend to be party animals
- romantics who pretend to be cynical
- sensitive souls who get off their faces so they can seem indifferent
- neurotics who pretend to be rebels
- men cast adrift.

What I know about their divorce, I only pieced together much later. My father spent too much time travelling, he was replaced. He told her about the times he was unfaithful, she took her revenge. The versions always differ: each blames the other so that to their children they can seem the innocent party. At the time, nothing was ever said, we had to guess, to learn to read between the lines without ever asking questions, smiling all the while in the silence of our invulnerable happiness. There was no yelling; the joy of life evaporated with the arrival of the Pill in the year that I was born – I made it into the world by the skin of my teeth.

Everyone was always right, everyone lied without meaning to because no one wanted to remember the precise truth, though it would have caused us less pain than how we saw things: our parents were bored of us. This life no longer suited them. Our family was no longer enough for them. The two blond brothers playing on the lawn were a disappointment, the game had ended too soon. Excitement was elsewhere, the times they were a-changing, it was now possible to be bourgeois and a hedonist, Catholicism no longer prohibited pleasure. Finally, people would be allowed to live less solemnly in a world in which sexual pleasure was an imperative. And what about the boys? They would tag along, they would survive. A divorce is not as serious as a world war. No one ever died from it; they won't complain. The boys were spoiled, they were showered with kisses and presents, Mako Mould and Paint sets, Mako Candle-Making sets, Chemistry 2000,* Lego, Meccano, Airfix soldiers and Märklin electric trains. Every weekend was Christmas, in an attempt to make up for the fact that we were entering into the new society mentioned by the prime minister with a voice like a duck (Jacques Chaban-Delmas), a consumer society of unlimited American luxury, a world in which loneliness could be alleviated with toys and ice-cream cones. Children were gorged to the point they were ruined. Divorced parents seemed younger than their tiresome children, like in *Absolutely*

*On the rue Monsieur-le-Prince, I mixed potassium permanganate with water: the mixture created a violently purple precipitate which spilled all over my schoolbag, stained my clothes and left brown streaks on my fingers for a month. These days, such toys are banned: potassium permanganate is classed as an explosive and a highly toxic substance. As you can see, from an early age I tinkered with illicit substances. (Note from an author who seems less and less amnesiac as his tale draws towards its conclusion.)

*Fabulous* where the daughter is constantly moralising to her alcoholic mother. It was in 1972 that the war between the generations ended: from this point people began to live as infantile individuals, as BFFs. The parents would forever be overgrown kids. The children would be grown-ups by the time they were eight, just like in movies of the period like *Bugsy Malone* or *La Petite*. My brother and I had not chosen this situation. But what happened, happened: in 1972, we witnessed our parents being born.

# 31

# PRISON BREAK

Compared to the Dépôt, the cells at the 8th arrondissement police station are like the Hôtel Ritz. My first night in prison was a bad joke, a game of cops and robbers, a schoolboy prank, like the drunken larks of the postal workers in the movie *Welcome to the Sticks*. The second night goes on a year, ten years, it is going on still. I knew nothing, I lived my whole life in ignorance. That night I realised that I had never known suffering. That place is a disgrace to this country, a hell much like La Santé Prison, where I had gone to visit the prisoners some years earlier after Véronique Vasseur had written a book denouncing the brutal conditions there: the book cost her her job as Chief Doctor at La Santé, but did nothing to change the disgusting conditions in the Paris prison. Le Dépôt, as the gaol attached to the Palais de Justice is known – is as oozing, as slimy and as cold as La Santé. The name is misleading – it's not a 'depository', it's a dungeon. Le Dépôt is a mass grave into which the cadaverous bodies of reprobates are cast. This particular dungeon dates from the Middle Ages, but you can still be banged up there. It is a vast underground gallery with thick walls, vaulted ceilings and two floors of cells fitted with thick bars and heavy metal doors with sliding bolts in which men scream for help, beg to be let out, declare their innocence and pound their heads against the bars. The Paris Dépôt is a miniature prison with about forty cells where those 'on remand' are held: the miscreants and the criminals the powers that be have deemed fit to incarcerate beneath the Palais de Justice until some judge deigns to wake up. You need only drink three glasses of wine and get behind the wheel of your car, take a toke on a spliff someone offers you, get picked up during a brawl or a demonstration, and if the judge or the cop is of a mind to, because you're famous or because he wants to make an example of you, or for the sheer sadistic pleasure because his wife didn't fuck him last night, you could wind up in the Dépôt on the Île de la Cité at the far end of a courtyard, underground, in the police station behind the Palais de Justice in the heart of the City of Light, a stone's throw from the Sainte-Chapelle, where you will be tossed, handcuffed, into a black hole, forced to strip again so they can check your arsehole before shoving you into a dank, freezing dungeon with no windows, a plank of wood for a bed, a squat toilet set into the floor, a zombie hutch with no heating where even the warders apologise with embarrassment and lower their eyes. A sympathetic officer, having recognised me shivering, curled into a foetal position, brought me two foul-smelling blankets. When I got bored learning by heart *Liaisons: The In-House Magazine of the Police Force* – the only reading material I was given after I begged – I screamed until the guard made a 4 a.m. appointment for me to see the on-call doctor so he could give me tranquillisers, because the state is a dealer, it hands out drugs for free, you just have to insist. I know what some readers will think: prissy little rich kid locked up in Marie-Antoinette's old prison cell! Well, if that's what you think, you've never been locked up. Anyone who has ever been in custody knows what I'm talking about: the return to the state of the shivering, cowering animal. And that's allowing for the fact that I got the VIP treatment, apparently, meaning I got my own cell, separated from the Poet and left to my panicked claustrophobia. The echoing footsteps and the muffled screams of the Dépôt will forever ring inside my head. The clank of chains, of keys, of handcuffs; the sound of sobs. The ice beneath the flagstones.

'It's not our fault, we haven't got the budget.' When we succumb to inhumanity, it's never anyone's fault. France managed to find billions of euros to bail out the banks in 2008, but it tolerates a HUMAN DUNGHEAP in the middle of Paris. The Commissioner for Human Rights at the Council of Europe denounced the conditions of this place in vain. There is a willingness at government level to preserve this brutal prison in the heart of our city. Someone took the rational decision to torture the people of France. France is a country that sanctions the use of torture in the 1st arrondissement, just opposite the fashionable department store La Samaritaine. And I would be colluding in this outrage if I did not depict it here. How can I have lived for forty-two years without taking an interest in this atrocity taking place in my own city? How can we dare presume to lecture China, Iran or Libya, when France has lost all self-respect? We have elected a president who spends his time freeing prisoners abroad and throwing people into dungeons at home. I remind my French readers that EVERY DAY people who are presumed innocent are locked up in a putrid freezing cesspit in THE COUNTRY THAT GAVE BIRTH TO HUMAN RIGHTS. I am talking about abject suffering taking place a short walk from the music bars of the place Saint-Michel, a short walk along the Seine from Lapérouse, where for three centuries aristocrats have gone for blow-jobs in private rooms, next to the Conciergerie where people shoot films and organise receptions (I remember dancing there one night in a tuxedo rented from Cor de Chasse at some fancy society ball), behind the Palais de Justice where I went twice in order to get my divorces, a few short steps from the exquisite place Dauphine where Yves Montand and Simone Signoret lived, yes, a few short steps from the home of those two great actors who spent their lives campaigning against such inhuman treatment, on an island in the Seine there is a place of torment lit up every night by the floodlights of the *bateaux mouches*, a squalid penitentiary, a sickening stain, a dank, bottomless pit, a freezing cellar where every night the cries of the wretched go unheeded, where sobs rise up to heaven every night God sends, TODAY, RIGHT NOW, AT THIS VERY MOMENT, IN THE CAPITAL OF FRANCE.*

*Since 2008 and my little rant in this chapter, the law has been changed in France such that people can no longer be banged up without recourse to legal representation. Meanwhile conditions in Le Depôt have been improved and the prison renovated. Perhaps literature is not completely ineffectual.

# 32

# DREAMS AND ILLUSIONS

I was very lucky; my parents had only one aim: not to traumatise their children. This was their obsession, their one rule of conduct. To protect their sons. Ensure that we did not come to hate our parents the way they hated theirs: our reactionary grandparents, penniless aristocrats and bourgeois eccentrics who had raised them in a harsh disciplinarian manner, locking them away in boarding schools, adhering to ideologies devoid of any tenderness, or raised them distractedly, being too distant and too prudish. When my parents divorced, my mother chose to hide the truth from her children, wrapping us in cotton wool. Rather than say, 'I'm leaving your father because I've fallen in love with another man,' she told us, 'Your father has a lot of work. He's in New York at the moment.'

I'm not criticising my mother for hiding the truth, but for inventing a lie that was less enthralling than the truth. She could simply have told us she was in love with someone else: *When Father was Away on Business* is not as moving as *Anna Karenina*. But my mother felt guilty for having fallen in love with a man other than my father. I'm angry with myself for having prompted that guilt. There's nothing wrong with falling out of love, still less with falling in love. I feel ashamed for having made my mother feel ashamed. Children want the impossible: they want nothing to ever change. They criticise their parents for being selfish when in fact they are the ones who are selfish. When I constantly pestered her to know where Papa was and why he had to work all the time, Maman would tell me everything was fine.

'When will he be back?'

'I don't know, poppet.'

The litany of happiness is suspect. We had just left a huge apartment on the avenue Henri-Martin and moved into a little two-bedroom place on the rue Monsieur-le-Prince. Even a six-year-old in a pair of New Man jeans can work out that his home has shrunk, that his father is never there. In the flat on the rue Monsieur-le-Prince, Maman taught us to brush our teeth, she put Mercurochrome on our cuts and scrapes, dried our blond hair and made Blédine with chocolate. Since I spent a lot of time watching

TV, I started watching American shows in the hope of seeing my father since he was 'working in New York'. I thought I might spot him on a street corner in some soap opera, see him coming out of a restaurant, climbing into a limo as he straightened his tie between important business meetings. New York brought me news of my overworked father. The white steam that rose from the gratings, the rusted fire escapes on the sides of buildings, the flickering neon signs of hotels, the police sirens, the suspension bridges . . . this was my father's home. My father was Mannix the detective, or the hero of *Mission Impossible* whose tape was always about to 'self-destruct in five seconds'. In my mind I travelled with him to an America where I had never been. I was a New Yorker like him; at night I dreamed of soaring, surreal skyscrapers, of walks where my father held my hand and took me to the cinema and we ate popcorn, hailed yellow cabs and I never minded having to wait for him in the lobby of some posh hotel or the air-conditioned hallway of some office block while he was in a business meeting. I was far from the rue Monsieur-le-Prince in this American movie that existed only in my head. A dream in the country of my grandmother Carthew-Yorstoun in which I had not lost my father. In my bed with its sheets depicting Mickey Mouse or Snoopy, I would make endless resolutions: next time Papa is home, I promise not to be a nuisance, not to bother him, cross my heart. Isn't that right Charles? We have to behave when Papa gets back or else he might go away again. Poor Charles, not only did he miss his father too, but sometimes I would keep him awake all night.

'Hey, Charles, are you asleep?'

'No, because you won't let me.'

(Silence.)

'Hey, Charles, are you asleep?'

'No, you just woke me up.'

(A longer silence.)

'Are you asleep now?'

'It would be more accurate to say I WAS asleep.'

'Charles? Do you think Papa will ever come back?'

'zzzzzzz.'

In wanting to spare their children, out of love, our parents taught us the art of not becoming attached. Taught us how to disguise our sadness and our regrets. They taught me to bottle up my pain: out of love, they taught me to be loveless; in trying to protect us they made us hard-hearted. It is possible that both my parents simultaneously suffered from depressions that went untreated. We are a family who never shouted at each other. My father and mother managed an extraordinary feat: they divorced without ever raising their voices. My mother never badmouthed my father; on the contrary, she would often say, 'Your father is the most intelligent man I ever met.'

My father never said a harsh word about my mother either, which simply made their separation more mysterious. We grew up in non-Aristotelian, a-human worlds, like the prisoners in the Dépôt. From an early age we learned to master our emotions, to become control freaks when it came to our hearts. Meaning that we never grew up, because we never understood. My adolescence rhymes with silence, absence, indifference. Ever since, I have been a torrent of emotions incapable of bursting its banks. What happened is now clear. For me there was no awkward age, no rebellion; my brother and I were model children, passed our baccalauréat at sixteen; we were well mannered, obedient, quietly miserable. Instead of getting tattoos and body piercings, we were happy to sit quietly watching Maritie and Gilbert Carpentier's variety show on TV, with sketches by Roger Pierre and Jean-Marc Thibault and appearances from Thierry Le Luron and Jacques Chazot. I'm going through my teenage angst right now: I've never been able to open up, I'm emotionally stunted, incapable of saying 'I love you'. Why is this family so determined to forever keep its silence? Discretion may be respectable, not so unending secrets and lies. In 1942, the children of this family knew nothing about the Jews sheltered by their parents on the second floor of the Villa Navarre; thirty years later, their children knew nothing about their own parents' divorce.

A child may be ignorant, but he is not blind. In attempting not to traumatise our children we traumatise them just the same, while they wait and hope for a reconciliation that never comes. It would be better to tell them straight that the death of love is irreversible.

# 33

# THE DISHONEST TRUTH

I can understand that my mother did not have the strength to tell us. When I left my daughter's mother, I too was a coward. It is very difficult to tell the child one loves that you are a romantic egoist. I would stare into her innocent eyes, hoping that they would remain so for as long as possible. Then came the fateful day when Chloë asked me the question all divorced parents dread: 'Papa, why don't you live with Maman any more?'

I said: 'Um . . . Because that's life . . . I will always love you, but with her it's complicated . . .'

'She says you used to go out every night, that you were really mean to her, and that's why she asked you to leave.'

'No, no . . . Well, yes . . . The fact is we argued a lot because of someone else . . .'

'Did you leave her for Amélie?'

'Yes . . .'

'And after that you left Amélie for Laura, and Laura for Priscilla?'

'Er . . . It's not that simple . . .'

'So you're like Bluebeard!'

'No! Bluebeard murdered his wives!'

'You're Bluebeard! My father is Bluebeard!'

In the end, when it comes to children, silence is almost the best solution. In the months that followed this conversation, I had to take my daughter to a child psychiatrist several times to get her to accept the idea that her father was not a monster who hung the corpses of his dead wives in cupboards. In a room strewn with brightly coloured toys, my daughter drew a house with a large mother inside and a tiny father outside, and I had to choke back my tears: this was my punishment for leaving her mother. My own mother never had to do such things: my brother and I went on smiling so that she would not feel guilty, and it was only forty years later that I decided to see a psychiatrist. At our last session, the shrink suffered shooting pains in her side at the end of my monologue. She collapsed on the floor and crawled, whimpering, from her consulting room to her library. Panicked, I asked her, 'What's the matter, doctor? Is it something I said?'

'Call my assistant, pleasaaaargh.'

I hope this book will not have the same effect

on all my readers. Our every action, our every word has consequences. My mother's silence about the sudden absence of my father meant that I lived out my whole childhood in a fiction in which my father was away on business and my neglected mother eventually found solace in the arms of another man. The opposite of the truth. I spent my childhood believing that my father had abandoned my mother, when in fact it was the reverse. Gradually, the official version became: 'Since your father is never around, we've decided to formalise our separation. Boys, this is Pierre.'

The stepfather my mother had chosen was an aristocrat with the same Christian name as her father. The Baron had Jean d'Ormesson's eyes and Robert Redford's wrinkles. We moved again, this time into a vast apartment in the rue de la Planche with bells in every room to summon the Mauritian manservant Saïdou, a tall black man who wore a white jacket. Today, after several decades of research and cross-checking worthy of Columbo, I can tell you that the true version of events is as follows: neglected by my father, my mother fell in love with one of his friends and went off with him, and my father was so miserable that he immersed himself in his work, in food, in women, taking on the role of CEO at his recruitment consultancy and putting on fifty kilos of excess weight. All childhoods may not be novels, but mine certainly is. It is a tragic novella, a failed love story of which my brother and I are the fruit. Ours was a Canada Dry happiness. A life that appeared to be happy: Neuilly, a posh neighbourhood, spacious villas in Pau, the beaches of Guéthary or Bali . . . it looks like happiness, it seems like happiness, but it's not happiness. You feel you should be happy, you're not happy, and so you pretend.

In a sense, it is the worst of all possible worlds: loving parents do everything in their power to make you happy, only to fail. They hate themselves, they do their best, and while they shower you with presents you feel ashamed that you cannot make them happy, ashamed to be sulking when – as the cop in the 8th arrondissement told me – you've got 'nothing to complain about'. My childhood is a little like those parties where you feel you should be having fun: everything is perfectly organised (there is more than enough to eat and drink, the music is great, the guests are good-looking and easy-going), but things simply do not gel. When I hear Chloë laughing as she blows bubbles, it always terrifies me. What if she too is only pretending to be happy so as not to disappoint me?

If you spend enough time pretending that there's no problem, you wind up with no memories.

# 34

# THE SECOND FATHER

After 1974 we lived out happy, forgotten days on the rue de la Planche. It's strange having a new father; you are not allowed to become attached. My father despised him. I felt I was not allowed to love this kindly baron in his striped seersucker suits who gave me presents, took me mackerel-fishing in Ireland, played jazz on his out-of-tune piano, entertained all of Castel in his vast white drawing room, danced the samba with my mother to the music of Jorge Ben every Sunday at the Brazilian brunches at Chez Guy on the rue Mabillon. We had to restrain ourselves from liking him for fear of another break-up (a fear that proved well founded). And yet it was at his place that Charles and I threw our first parties five years later, where Charles endlessly played Patti Smith's 'Because the Night' and I endlessly played 'One Step Beyond' by Madness. We spent so much time dancing to ska in the dining room that the soles of our shoes left black streaks on the white parquet floor. We danced with such frenzy all our friends left with armpit stains. My new father was the man my first father was trying to become. A playboy – he had dated the singer Jeane Manson – and businessman – he worked for Antoine Riboud, the CEO of BSN Gervais-Danone. I remember that the great man used to come to our house with pockets full of Carambar, and once he had us test his newest innovation, the Evian atomiser spray. The Baron's friends were called Pierre Bouteiller, Mort Schuman, Thierry Nicolas, Pierre de Plas, Olivier de Kersauson and Jean-Pierre Ramsay. He was witty, handsome, at ease in any situation, unfailingly courteous and gentle. My mother was surrounded by elegant female friends: Sabine Imbert, the Petitjean sisters (granddaughters of the founder of Lancôme), Princess Michael of Kent, Guillemette de Sairigné, Béatrice Pepper . . . She was happier than she ever had been while she was married. Deep down, the Baron epitomised everything that my mother scorned before 1968 (urbane, frivolous, *bon vivant*); and yet he was my second father. Though he was older, he spent as many years raising me as my real father; but I felt like a traitor living in his house, felt disloyal seeing him embrace my mother, being a witness to this love that caused my first father so much pain. I was not his son, so what was I doing in the home of this man who spoiled me more than my noble progenitor? Had I the right to love this man who had replaced my father? It's certainly obvious that I have spent a good part of my life following in his footsteps. It was he who first took me to Castel, where I had a bottle in my own name at the age of thirteen – the memory of glittering women like precious jewels nestling on a cushion of smoke. I fell in love with the night, because everything about it was artificial and magical. I loved the synthetic beauty of this imaginary country. My mother's lover opened the door to this enchanting fiction where people laugh too loudly, where women are more beautiful by night, music more resonant. Noticing that I paid close attention to his set list, the DJ at Castel gave me a tape which I still listen to sometimes in the radio-cassette player in my father's old BMW, the only device on which I can still listen to cassettes: Kraftwerk's 'Radioactivity' cross-fading into 'Speak to Me/ Breathe' by Pink Floyd. I still think it is the most beautiful segue in the world.

My new father never became my stepfather (he never married Maman), but he was a sort of 'antifather'. I remember him scribbling a conundrum – 'Pierre/2' – on a napkin over lunch at Claude Sainlouis on the rue du Dragon: '/2' represented his surname: *deux sous le trait* = de Soultrait. At the time, all I could think of was 'divided in two'. Now I realise that the situation was banal: all children feel divided. This is how life is born: cells are created by the process of cell division (*omnis cellula ex cellula*); it is cell multiplication that keeps an organism alive. When my second father disappeared from my life in 1980, the first reappeared more frequently, and after that I only ran into the Baron once or twice by chance in restaurants in Bidart or on the rue de Varenne. New families are temporary structures; from an early age I learned to watch those closest to me vanish overnight. My succession of stepfathers and my interchangeable stepmothers made it possible for me to experience individualism in the flesh. I acquired a prodigious aptitude, a gift for forgetting: amnesia as precocious talent and strategy for survival.

My father always resented the Baron for stealing his wife. One day, when I was grown up, I asked the $64,000 question: 'But since you were cheating on Maman, didn't she have the right to do the same thing?'

'It's not the same thing. She betrayed me, with

a friend. Besides, adultery is not as serious for a man.'

This line of reasoning is often used by men to justify their adultery. It is notably present in Schopenhauer: 'Adultery on the part of the woman is much less pardonable than on the part of the man, both objectively on account of the consequences and also subjectively on account of its unnaturalness.' This famous argument from *The World as Will and Representation* clearly did not convince my mother in 1972. I often attempted to trot it out during my later conjugal set-tos: 'Darling, if I am cheating on you, it's not as serious because I'm a man. And that's not me talking, that's Arthur Schopenhauer.'

Two divorces later, I can now confirm based on experience that this entails an AFC (Argument from Codology).

At some point (the Passy-Buzenval episode), I have the impression that my father experienced the absurd fear of being eclipsed by his successor. I remember the night when he came round to my mother's to take his sons for the weekend, and rather than kiss him, I held out my hand to shake his. It was an unconscious act of rebellion aimed at his unexplained disappearance: offering my spiteful little hand as to a stranger rather than my soft cheek. I was ten years old, and yet even today I am appalled at my cruelty that night. Naturally my father reacted very badly; he was hurt, and forcibly kissed me. I feel as though I have been unfair to this man my whole life. I genuinely believed he had deserted us. I have often tried to write about him: the hero of *Windows on the World* has trouble looking after his two sons, and bears the surname of my American grandmother . . . At one point he says to his boys: 'There are worse things in life than having an absent father: having a present father. Some day you'll thank me for not smothering you. You'll realise I was helping you find your wings, pampering you from afar.' Books are a way of talking to those to whom we cannot talk.

To tell my father how I feel, I would probably do better to quote another American movie, Alexander Payne's *About Schmidt* (2002). Jack Nicholson plays Warren Schmidt, a sixty-six-year-old retired, cynical, bitter, lonely widower with a pot belly and a tweed cap who writes to a small boy in Tanzania named Ndugu. Every month Schmidt sends him $22 to fund his education, and he confides in him. The voiceover of Schmidt's letters to Ndugu, the distant boy he sponsors without ever meeting, forms the main thread of the story. At the end of the film, the Mother Superior in charge of Ndugu's school in Africa sends Mr Schmidt a drawing in which the boy has tried to express what his penpal means to him. From the envelope Jack Nicholson takes a piece of paper, a childlike drawing of a smiling man holding the hand of a child who is also smiling beneath a huge, dazzling sun. When he sees it, Schmidt bursts into tears.

# 35

# THE END OF AMNESIA

I was locked up in a lie. When I realised that my amnesia stemmed from something left unsaid, everything suddenly appeared before me on the wall of my rathole; it was as though dawn were breaking, as though a curtain were being drawn on my childhood, now once again free. Everything, I remembered everything: riding a tricycle in the square hallway in Neuilly; the duplex in the 16th arrondissement where I heard of the death of de Gaulle and tasted my first cherries; the fights with my brother over the blue eggcup and the pointed spoon; the huge box of multi-coloured Caran d'Ache markers I used to draw trees on the wallpaper in my bedroom; listening to the LP of Gérard Philipe reading *The Little Prince* and thinking this was the prince who had given his name to the street we lived on; my first burger at a McDonald's on the corner of the rue Monsieur-le-Prince and the boulevard Saint-Michel, which was renamed

O'Kitch when they lost the franchise; the noise of our Matchbox cars in the hall, which annoyed the downstairs neighbours; the Kids' Club with Mathieu Cocteau on the big beach at Guéthary where Monsieur Rimbourd had us sing 'We are the ducks, the sweet little ducks, the happy little ducks who have plenty of pluck'; Barnaby the Bear who sings his way to fame; the swimming pool at the Hôtel Lutetia where the gym teacher from the Lycée Bossuet took us swimming every week (these days it's a clothes shop); and Zoom the White Dolphin; and the games of Mille Bornes when it rained at Patrakénéa; the wind that slammed the shutters against the white-washed wall; my little blue plastic Pez dispenser with a Popeye head that opened to spit out bland sweets as I huddled under the bedsheets in the middle of a thunderstorm; the stuffed beaver brought back from Yosemite National Park that got singed on the bulb of my bedside lamp; the day my father was furious because Charles and I dashed up to our apartment to open his magic boxes and forgot to wave to him from the window to let him know we'd got in safely; listening to the Gilbert O'Sullivan single 'Get Down' with Henri de la Celle at his home, Château Elyas; and the era when armchairs and lamps looked like bubbles; and

Caranougat bars; and the day I saw Sartre having lunch alone at the Brasserie Balzar; and the ads for the Playtex eighteen-hour girdle ('Where did I put my girdle? Oh, I forgot, I've got it on!'); *Daktari* with Clarence the lion; and 'Changing your outfit? Change to a Kelton watch!'; and the cartons of Nestlé sweetened condensed milk in the fridge in Verbier; and the fat paedo neighbour on the top floor of the rue de la Planche who invited me into his *chambre de bonne* to suck sugar balls . . . Huh? What? What did I say?

The *chambres de bonne* in the apartment block on the rue de la Planche were a bad idea. Much as I liked the rubbish chute, into which I used to throw sugar lumps to listen to them clattering to the bottom, the studio flats on the top floor brought us bad luck. To get there you had to take the back stairs from the seventh floor under the attic. These tiny two-room flats were our playrooms, our secret hideaways as adolescents. Charles once burned his arm there while conducting a scientific experiment with a friend (the experiment made it possible for them to conclude that methylated spirit is inflammable). And I used to run into this fat guy who would play with his dick and compliment me on my silken hair. I never gave in to the advances of the libidinous old man. Thankfully I didn't find him attractive. Otherwise by now I might be Marc Dutroux.

# 36

## THE DAY I BROKE MY MOTHER'S HEART

'Give Mama a little kiss, poppet.'

'Maman, I'm forty-two. Could you please stop calling me poppet?'

'Oh, I'm sorry, Frédéric. What am I thinking? I'm sorry . . .'

'No, look, it's OK, Maman, it's not a problem. I was just saying . . .'

A mother does not notice her son growing old, especially if he refuses to grow up. When I was about a month old I liked having my neck kissed. When I was thirteen, my mother suggested I should stop coming into my stepfather's bed to snuggle with her. I still remember the day she rebuffed me: we had just been watching Louis Malle's film *La Souffle au coeur* on television, the story of a son who sleeps with his mother. I was sitting in my pyjamas next to my own mother; the film was broadcast with a small white 'adults only' warning rectangle on the bottom right-hand corner of the screen; the embarrassment was mutual and mute. It was time for her to become a woman like any other, meaning a woman who refused to allow me to kiss her. Until that morning in the bed on the rue de la Planche when she explained to me that I was too big now to kiss her neck, my mother was the only woman who had never rebuffed my advances. I have never kissed anyone more than I did her. Thirteen years of uninterrupted affection: none of the women who came after her ever beat that record. Even today, I spend much of my time with my face buried in the long, tender, perfumed necks of women. It has always been the place on earth where I feel happiest.

Some months after this maternal rejection, my mother announced to my brother and me that we were moving again. My stepfather did not want to marry her. They no longer got along; they were splitting up because they were constantly arguing. Theirs had been a passionate love affair: living together had snuffed it out. Half-heartedly, we assented, as always, before packing up our boxes. Break-ups succeeded each other, resembled each other: we moved into a small three-room apartment on the rue Coëtogon in the 6th arrondissement, then Giscard lost the election to Mitterrand. A few weeks passed. I don't remember how I found out that my ex-stepfather had married another woman in Reno (Nevada) on a whim. One evening out of the blue, while we were eating dinner in the kitchen, I asked my mother, 'Did you know Pierre got married? He went to America with a girlfriend and married her.'

I have never seen anyone crumple so completely. Maman went pale; she got up from the table, stalked out and slammed the door. Charles congratulated me on my gaffe.

'Bravo! Full marks for tact!'

'Well, I didn't know that she didn't know.'

My uncle Bertrand was determined to smash the Baron's face; I don't know whether he did. Perhaps these pathetic farces are important only to those who lived through them. This little world has long since been reconciled, but to break your mother's heart – however unwittingly – is something that I would not wish on anyone. Every time there was some drama in her life on the rue Coëtlogon, my mother's voice on the phone would drop to a whisper and she would switch to speaking English so we would not realise that her new boyfriend was marrying someone else, had thrown himself out of a window, or couldn't bring himself to leave his wife because she had cancer. Charles and I knew only too well that whenever she left the living room, tugging on the phone cord, we were in for a night of listening to her sniffling and blowing her nose. She slaved away translating soppy romantic novels, working for peanuts just so there would be food in the fridge and we would not go without. The glorious life of a liberated woman: get up at 7 a.m., make the children's breakfast, check their schoolbags, work until 6 p.m. for some vile boss or sweat blood over a shitty manuscript that needs to be completely rewritten to be able to pay for rent, food, clothes, holidays and taxes, pick the kids up from study at 7 p.m., feed them veal escalope and Maron Sui's chestnut mousse, make sure they do their homework, try to stop them fighting, get them to bed at a reasonable hour. We were not exactly rolling in money, despite the alimony my father paid and my mother's meagre pittance of a salary. We had experienced the same discrepancy when we moved onto the rue Monsieur-le-Prince and, for my tenth birthday, I asked for an encyclopaedia. I wasn't expecting her to get me the *Universalis*! I only wanted a children's reference book. Since the *Encyclopaedia Universalis* was too expensive, I got volumes A–F on 21 September 1975, then had to wait for

Christmas for volumes F–M. The following year, I was given volumes M–Z. Maybe I'm ridiculous, but it breaks my heart when I remember my mother's disconsolate face as she apologised for not being able to afford to give me the encyclopaedia all at once.

To be a single woman raising two children is like serving a prison sentence. I later learned what it means to be a single mother: she is someone who gives life to you only to sacrifice her own. She left our father, then our stepfather, and from that moment on she never stopped trying to expiate the faults for which we did not blame her. She had decided to be an independent woman, that is to say a saint like her grandfather who committed suicide during the First World War. I know that many writers feel a resentment towards their mother. For my part, I feel only gratitude. Her love was boundless. She must have realised that we, at least, would never leave her; and in that she was mistaken. I remember, I brought her back a T-shirt from the United States that made her laugh: 'I survived a Catholic mother'. Our mother's love was so possessive that it was almost painful. Her love constantly apologised for loving. It was a love that could make you depressed, since it felt as though it were compensating for some emptiness. My brother and I exploited our mother's doomed love life and the slavery of feminism – before this, women raised the children; now they raise children and ON TOP OF THAT they have to work. Freed of the chains of marriage and a relationship, she worked in publishing, raised her children single-handed, and I do not believe that she was happy. I was a boy subject to a new matriarchy, one who idolised his mother but took my revenge on other women. My childhood left me a creature who hungered for women's bodies with a vengeful misogyny. My mother had only us, and we took full advantage: we had a liberated stay-at-home mother. We had won the battle of love against all her other men. Our childhood ended with our mother becoming our slave. We tested out a new neurosis: the competitive Oedipus complex, in which two boys mercilessly exploit a single mother. I still wonder if it is our fault that she lives alone to this day.

# 37

# PARENTAL INVENTORY

*Things I get from my mother:*

- *Elton John's ballads from 1969 to 1975, the pinnacle of international pop music*
- *always seeing a Woody Allen movie on the day it is released*
- *the best red wine is not necessarily the most expensive*
- *discontentment, constant complaining, never being happy with anything*
- *short-sightedness*
- *romanticism*
- *my slight build*
- *a good education*
- *blushing*
- *snobbery*
- *knowing how to dress well*
- *liking my own company*
- *not being afraid to break up with someone*
- *Russian writers*

– *eating* foie gras *with a fork*
– *independence*
– *not being ashamed to cry in public* or *in front of the TV*
– *an inferiority complex*
– *roast leg of lamb with garlic*
– *being kissed on the neck*
– *a keen critical approach*
– *gentleness to others, cruelty to oneself*
– *a taste for gossip*
– Singin' in the Rain *by Gene Kelly and Stanley Donen*
– *long lie-ins with breakfast in bed, the smell of toast in the morning*
– *love should be passionate, unconditional, intense, possessive, even if that means it is short-lived*
– *love trumps everything else in existence*
– *never saying 'this lunchtime'*
– *a passion for reading.*

*Things I get from my father:*

– *extravagance*
– *delusions of grandeur*
– *a big nose*
– *frequent sore throats*

- *my protruding chin*
- *eyes the colour of rain*
- *a habit of sneezing twice very loudly and terrifying the whole house*
- *a love for* fondue bourguignonne *and* fondue savoyarde
- *clear-sightedness*
- *Brooks Brothers*
- *sarcasm*
- *egotism*
- *sexual addiction*
- *saying 'brogues' for 'shoes', 'sweater' for 'jumper' and 'the funnies' for 'comics'*
- *a sense of occasion*
- *a love of open fires*
- *a taste for younger women*
- *the Marx Brothers*
- *Monteverdi's* Vespro della Beata Vergine
- *not giving a toss for other people's opinions*
- *the soundtrack of* American Graffiti
- *a superiority complex*
- *tropical islands*
- *doing my shopping at the Duty Free*
- *it is possible to eat a whole* saucisson *in less than five minutes*
- *being permanently laid-back but sometimes getting worked up over something trivial*

– *snoring*
– *a solipsism worthy of Plotinus*
– *shamelessness is a virtue*
– *a passion for writing.*

# 38

## THE FRENCH DREAM

My father never celebrated his own birthdays, and often forgot those of his sons. He did not bother to remember the dates, understandably deeming that he had already given us the greatest possible gift: life. This disciple of ancient philosophy considered reality to be relative: consequently it was senseless to accord much importance to a date on the calendar symbolising the biological ageing process. The refusal to grow up is part of my heritage, together with the idea that reality is an overrated concept.

After his divorce, my father found himself an ersatz big brother, a substitute elder sibling in the person of Jean-Yves Beigbeder. I remember a more heavyset double of my father with thick glasses, a guy who was funny, whimsical, freethinking, unique, like the man my father would later become. We all went on holidays together to the British West Indies, to a little island called Nevis, though I have no memory of the trip aside from my discovery of coconut milk. Later, it was surely out of nostalgia for Nevis that I misspent my youth eating Bounty bars and drinking Malibu. One day our father announced in a funereal voice that Jean-Yves Beigbeder was dead, drowned or devoured by sharks off the Great Barrier Reef. I too have a friend who bears the same first names, but he does not wish to be mentioned here – oops . . . too late!

My father experienced the capitalist dream and my mother the feminist utopia, and both were severely punished for wanting their freedom. '*Calamitosus est animus futuri anxius*,' as Seneca says ('Dreadful the mind that is fearful of the future'). But there is one thing that no one can take from them: at least my parents had a dream.

# 39

# COMPULSIVE LIARS

I understand now: the beach at Guéthary is me holding my breath so as not to remember Paris. My indiscretions and my nocturnal excesses: distractions so as not to have to write this book. I have spent my whole life avoiding writing this book.

It is the story of a Seventies Emma Bovary who, when she divorced, replicated the silence of the previous generation about the horrors of two world wars.

It is the story of a man who became a playboy to revenge himself for being dumped, of a father who became cynical because his heart was broken.

It is the story of an older brother who did everything he could not to be like his parents, and a younger brother who did everything he could not to be like his big brother.

It is the story of two children who ended up fulfilling the dreams of their parents to avenge their disappointed love.

It is the story of a boy who was melancholy because he grew up in a country that was slowly committing suicide, raised by parents depressed by the failure of their marriage.

It is the story of the death of the cultured provincial upper-middle classes and the disappearance of the values of the old chivalrous aristocracy.

It is the story of a country that managed to lose two wars and pretend that they had won, and went on to lose its colonial empire while behaving as though this made no difference to its importance.

It is the story of a new humanity, or how monarchist Catholics became globalised capitalists.

This is the life I have led: a French novel.

# 40

# RELEASE

It was a shaggy-haired zombie with foul breath, stiff legs and a rumpled jacket that the police came and placed once again in handcuffs two days after his initial arrest. Torn from a numb, frozen half-sleep, I was sneezing, my nose was running, and I was suffering the effects of the Valium and the beta-blockers dispensed by the duty doctor and the court-appointed lawyer. I had, as Blondin writes in *Monsieur Jadis ou l'École du Soir* (1970), 'the mangy look of mornings after a night in the slammer'. Released from my metal fridge, I followed an uncommunicative automaton who walked through the oozing underground corridors beneath a ceiling trailing pipes and electric cables lit by bare, sometimes broken bulbs; flanked by uniformed officers I stumbled along, shackled beneath the earth. I was shoved into a different cell with two other prisoners who were doing their best to reassure each other; I must have slept for a few minutes, squatting, sitting, sprawling, unheeded; then came the longest seconds in my life, the moment when I most desperately missed my pen. Pencils and pens are forbidden in the Dépôt, since they risk being plunged into someone's eye, their cheek, their belly – too much temptation. I was trying not to worry about the verdict of the judge whose devastating power I had experienced over the past thirty-six hours. A great criminal lawyer, Maître Caroline Toby, called by one of the witnesses to my arrest, came and took me out of the cell and explained the situation in no uncertain terms: should the slightest tic irritate the Vice-Procureur – a raised eyebrow, a stifled cough, a hint of sarcasm – then this woman I did not know could continue to crush me as she saw fit, with no possibility of appeal or debate, by sending me for immediate trial before a magistrates' court where I would be viewed as the epitome of a ne'er-do-well in need of a sharp lesson, an insolent penpushing junky punishable by one year in prison (according to article L. 3421-1 of the Public Health Code). I felt as grimy as the walls and the floor. I thought about my mother, about my daughter, about my fiancée, about how to lie to them, what excuse to give when news of the case got into the papers. 'Maybe I could tell them I ran a red light, or drove the wrong way down a one-way street . . .?' The lawyer explained that the prosecutor would alert the media, something she did in fact make sure to do: the following day I was on the front page of *Le Parisien*, because this is the double jeopardy reserved for criminals who do not have the good fortune to be anonymous. I would probably not have written this book if the French judicial system had not first made the case public. The glacial prosecutor I eventually met in the tiny office strewn with case files asked me a curious question: 'Do you know why you are here?'

I bitterly regret that my retort was that of a shivering zombie! I should have asked her if she knew what a 'Sprouzo' was (a cocktail of Sprite and Ouzo commonly imbibed around the Aegean). She would have said 'No', and I would then have said, 'I'm afraid it's impossible for us to understand each other, Madame. I haven't eaten anything for two days. I've lost three kilos. You have tortured me despite the fact that I am not a terrorist, a murderer, a rapist or a thief, and that any harm I do, I do only to myself. The moral principles that led you to inflict such violence on me are a thousand times less important than those you have flouted over the past two nights. (Then, in a low voice) I need to tell you a secret. My ID card says that I am forty-two years old, but in actual fact I am only eight. Do you understand? You have to let me out of here, because it is against the law to keep an eight-year-old child in custody. I am not as old as my documents maintain. Did my life somehow slip away? I didn't see it pass. I am completely immature. I am puerile, easily led, incompetent, thoughtless, naïve: a babe in arms – and you tell me I am an adult who should face up to my responsibilities? Listen, you've got the wrong man! Someone will clear up this misunderstanding.

But I was shaking like a leaf, with cold and with fear: I had lost all eloquence. I mumbled that I was sorry, Madame. That for two days I had gone from one disappointment to another. I wanted to be able to reassure my daughter, who I had not been able to pick up from school on Tuesday evening, that I had had my fill of false hopes and of time refusing to pass. France had won the battle against one of her sons. The magistrate ordered a drug rehabilitation programme, and I heaved a sigh of relief and meekly hung my head. I signed a few administrative autographs in order to get back my belongings, which had been rolled into a ball in a box in the basement. After that I had a meeting with a psychiatrist sitting between two Marilyn Manson clones with sunken cheeks. The Poet had disappeared, but I later found out from Maître Toby that he had received the same sentence: no police record, all charges dismissed in exchange for an undertaking to attend six sessions with a Creole psychologist on the rue Saint-Lazare. I finally stepped out of my medieval prison into the chill winter sunshine. I walked along the Seine, crossed the Pont-Neuf and phoned someone I loved.

'Hello, don't worry, I'll tell you everything, I got arrested with the Poet and I've spent the past thirty-six hours locked up, I haven't slept, I stink, I spent the whole night trembling with cold and claustrophobia, I have to go and feed the cat right now, she must be dying of starvation. No, I couldn't call earlier, they confiscated my mobile and I only had the right to one phone call to let Delphine know that I wouldn't be able to pick Chloë up from school the day before yesterday. Oh, come on darling, don't get upset, everything will be fine, I'm closing a chapter of non-life. I'd like you to console me. Could you come over to my place? Don't forget to bring your two arms, I plan to sleep in them. Oh, and I love you. And do you know what? It's just possible that I might finally be a man now.

# 41

## NEW YORK, 1981 OR 1982

Before heading to Guéthary, I went to New York for a week. One morning, on the phone, Jay McInerney told me he'd broken his foot tripping on the pavement on 9th Street at six in the morning and that it was all my fault because I had dragged him to the Beatrice Inn the night before and left him there in very unsavoury company. I always get the blame; I'm responsible for all the ills of the world, but I'm used to it, I'm Catholic. Then again, I spent thirty-six hours in prison for imitating Jay in *Lunar Park*. Let us consider his broken foot to be the application of a sort of *lex talionis* in transatlantic literary fiction. We often do apartment swaps (Jay comes to live at my place in Paris and I stay in his place in New York), the least we can do is swap misfortunes. I hang up, and suddenly I have a revelation: my first memories as an adult take place in New York. Out of the blue, a flood of New York memories rise to the surface, shifting, jostling, superimposing, merging. New York is my second city, the one where I've lived longest after Paris. When I was a teenager, my uncle George Harben would put me up in his apartment on Riverside Drive. I had the keys to his place, I came home whenever I liked, I had a staggering amount of freedom for a young man of sixteen who hadn't yet lost his cherry. Earlier still, I had spent summers at American 'summer camps' learning to play tennis from Nick Bollettieri and the lyrics to 'Dust in the Wind'. George died this year; ungrateful brat that I am, I didn't even go to his funeral. Later, my father bought a loft with a vast picture window in Museum Tower on 53rd Street just above MoMA. I organised after-parties there with Alban de Clermont-Tonnerre when we stumbled out of the Area, or the Limelight, or Nell's. My father had to sell the apartment when his brother put the family business into voluntary liquidation. My memories mingle like a Long Island Iced Tea. The first club I ever went to alone, on the rooftop, under the stars, was called the Danceteria. I tried my best to come on like John Lurie, the sax player with the Lounge Lizards. I wore Burlington socks and a pair of brown Sebago dress shoes. I remember the fashion then was for partying on the rooftops. We went to the Latino nights every Wednesday at Windows on the World: my first caipirinhas. Visions of New York like multiple exposures in a film. Speeded-up clouds scud by symbolising the passage of time. I first loved New York because there I could be alone. For the first time in my life, I could go where I wanted, pass myself off as someone else, dress differently, lie to strangers, sleep by day and hang about at night. New York encourages teenagers the world over to rebel like Holden Caulfield: not being obliged to go home is a form of utopia. When asked for your name, give a false identity. Narrating a life other than one's own is the least a budding novelist should be able to do. I even had a fake ID made on 42nd Street so I could pretend I was of legal age. New York is the city that persuaded me that I was going to write, meaning that I would finally be able to free myself from myself (at least that's what I thought at the time), to pass myself off as someone else, to become Marc Marronnier or Octave Parango, a fictional hero. It was here I turned out my first short story ('An Outmoded Text'). It was here I invented the person that for the past twenty years people have mistaken for me. There were a handful of us, living in empty apartments, experiencing our first summer of freedom. We were drunken teenagers ligging around the city, we copped an attitude more often than we copped a feel, we headed home at five in the morning in taxis drunker than we were, we shivered on Avenue A stumbling out of the Pyramid. Back then New York was still a dangerous city full of whores, drag queens and dealers. We lived for the thrills, we liked to think of ourselves as men, but we didn't do drugs – other than poppers. By my calculations, this would have been in 1981 or 1982. I'd buy records at Tower Records on Broadway. It closed recently, a victim of music downloading. We'd go and throw rice at the Waverly Theatre in Greenwich Village which had a midnight screening of *The Rocky Horror Picture Show* every Saturday. That cinema is long gone too. So many things in New York have disappeared . . . I lived on hot dogs, pretzels, Bubble Yum and Doritos dipped in guacamole. A lost and happy hellion . . . a self-made orphan. One morning – I remember this as clear as day – I realised I had grown up, that I was shopping for my dinner, that I had become an adult before turning eighteen. My childhood ends that morning. I was an adult in a child's body; then, one fine morning, I became a child in an adult's body. The only difference: as a child I often saw the sun set; as an adult I often see it rise. Dawns are less serene than dusks. How many more of them are left to me?

# 42

# RESULTS

Time flown cannot be regained; it is impossible to relive a disappeared childhood. And yet . . .

The tale I have told here is not necessarily the reality, but my childhood as I perceived it, as I have hesitantly recreated it. Everyone has different memories. This reinvented childhood, this recreated past is now my only truth. Since what is written becomes truth, this novel recounts my real life, which will no longer change and which, from now on, I will no longer forget.

I have filed away my memories here as in a cupboard. They will not move from here. I will no longer see them other than in these words, these images in this particular order; I have frozen them just like, as a child, I played with Mako Mould and Paint, sculpting characters with quick-setting plaster.

Everyone assumes that I have often written about my life, when in fact I have only just begun. I would like them to read this novel as though it were my first. Not that I disown my previous work; on the contrary, I hope that in time readers will come to see that . . . blah blah blah. But up until now I have depicted a man I am not, the man I would have liked to be, the arrogant lothario that the uptight posh boy in me fantasises about. I believed sincerity was boring. This is the first time I have tried to free someone long shut away.

It is possible to write the way Houdini cast off his bonds. Writing can serve as a developer, in the photographic sense of the term. This is why I love autobiography: it seems to me that, somewhere buried within us, there is an adventure that longs only to be discovered, and which, if we can only unearth it, is the most amazing story ever told. 'One day my father met my mother and then I was born and I lived my life.' Wow, it's crazy when you think about it. The rest of the world probably doesn't give a fuck, but this is our own private fairy tale. Granted, my life is no more interesting than yours, but it is no less interesting either. It is just a life, and the only one I have. If there is a chance in a million that this book will make my father, my mother and my brother immortal, then it was worth writing.

It is as though from this sheaf of pages I have created a billboard that reads: 'FROM NOW ON, NO ONE LEAVES ME'.

No one in this book will ever die.

An image that was invisible appeared to me suddenly in these pages just as, when I was a little boy, I would place a blank piece of paper on top of a one-franc piece and rub it with a pencil and see the figure of *La Semeuse* – the figure of a woman sowing seeds – in all her translucent splendour.

# 43

# THE A IN ATLANTIS

In those days, France was governed by a man who believed that religion gave life meaning. Is this the reason that he organised this hell? This ridiculous misadventure resembles a Catholic parable. The pathetic episode with the coke on the bonnet opened up new horizons for me like the apple falling on Newton's head. I decided to stop being someone else. They want me to play the prodigal son, they want me to come home? I become myself, but make no mistake, I will never follow the straight and narrow. The Dépôt was my Gehenna. Now that I have been damned, all that is left is for me to believe. The most Catholic thing about me is this: I prefer my pleasures to be forbidden. I did not deserve to be publicly humiliated, but I now know that I will always take the risk. I will always be beyond your control. You have declared war on me. I will never be one of you; I have chosen the other camp. 'I feel utterly comfortable in my withering,'

Baudelaire wrote to Hugo after *Les Fleurs du mal* was banned. Do not believe me when I smile at you, beware of me, I am a spineless kamikaze, I lie to you in a cowardly fashion, I am irredeemable, I am spoiled rotten, rotten in the sense of a tooth that is beyond saving. When I think that people call me a socialite when in fact I have been asocial since 1972 . . . True, I wear a jacket and tie and my shoes were shined yesterday by the staff at a Parisian palace. And yet still I am not one of you. I am descended from a hero who died for France, so if I commit hara-kiri myself for you, it's only because it runs in the family. This is the duty of soldiers as it is of writers. In my family, we kill ourselves for your sake without being one of you.

These were my rambling thoughts as I watched my brother being awarded the Légion d'honneur in the Salle des Fêtes of the Élysée Palace shortly after my release from the Dépôt. My mother was wearing red earrings, my father a blue suit. As the President of the Republic was pinning the medal to Charles's chest, my godchild Émilie, his three-year-old daughter, exclaimed, 'Maman, I need to go poo-poo.' The President pretended not to hear this anarchist outburst. To judge by appearances, we seemed a close-knit family.

Leaning against a gilded column, I ran my fingers through my hair. It's become a tic; I often do it when I don't know what to do with my hands. As I straightened my hair I surreptitiously scratched my head. Cold misted the windows that look out onto the grounds of the palace. I walked over and stared out at the trees, then suddenly, proudly, I drew the letter 'A' with my index finger on the frosty pane.

# EPILOGUE

These days my nose no longer bleeds the way it did when, at the age of seven, I thought I was going to die. In Guéthary, I snort salt sea air. Two weeks after my release from the Dépôt, the Rhune carves out its mountainous blue behind me. To my left, the Pyrenees tumble into the ocean. To my right, the water is so cold that the cliff has retreated: the Atlantic erodes and terrifies it. In two metres, I will be a hundred years old. My aunt Marie-Sol told me that from here, in 1936, you could see the town of Irun burning in the night, set ablaze by the *Republicanos* during the Spanish Civil War. Then the war came to France and my grandfather lost it. I walk along the rocky beach of Cénitz in February 2008, my daughter's hand in mine. The sea spray is my Evian atomiser. Sadly, local by-laws mean that since 2003 shrimp-fishing has been forbidden. This was never my favourite beach, yet today I am trembling with joy. The tide is out; on her spindly, never-ending legs, my daughter bounds from rock to rock like a kid goat. A goat dressed in a beige down jacket and a pair of suede boots singing '*Laisse tomber les filles*' by France Gall. A goat that sometimes asks philosophical questions:

'Papa?'

'Yes?'

'Do you prefer to believe, to think or to imagine?'

'What?'

'Do you say "I believe that", "I think that", or "I imagine that"?'

'Um . . . "I imagine that". It sounds more modest.'

'So you prefer to imagine.'

'Rather than thinking or believing, yes. It's easier.'

Thirty-six years earlier, on the afternoon of my solitary memory, my grandfather taught me something else besides how to fish for shrimp: he also taught me to skim stones.

'The most important thing,' he insisted, 'is to choose the right stone. It has to be round and flat. Look.'

There was no one on the beach but us on that one day I remember. Pierre de Chasteigner crouched down behind me to demonstrate the perfect posture, facing the sea, his arm following through with mine, the way golf and tennis coaches do. The white-haired war veteran had the time to show his scrawny grandson how to skim stones so they bounced across the water.

'You half turn your body so you'll have some momentum. That's right, like that. And then, *hop*, you release the stone.'

Splash.

'No, no, Frédéric, that one was too heavy.'

My stone had sunk miserably to the bottom of the ocean, carving ripples in the black water like the grooves on a record. My grandfather encouraged me to try again.

'But . . . Bon Papa, skimming stones is pointless.'

'On the contrary, it's very important. The point is to defy gravity.'

'Gravity?'

'Normally, if you throw a stone into the sea, it sinks to the bottom. But if you angle it at twenty degrees and aim your stone well, you can win a victory over gravity.'

'You still lose, just more slowly.'

'Exactly.'

This is something my grandfather taught me.

I no longer had nosebleeds, or at least I no longer thought about it. He patiently corrected my stance.

'Look at me. You have to swing like the Diskobolus.'

'What's a discobobulus?'

'It's a Greek statue. Don't worry. Just act like you're throwing a discus.'

'Something like a Frisbee, you mean?'

'What's a Frisbee?'

'You know . . . the round thing we throw to each other on the beach . . .'

'Stop interrupting me! OK, you pivot like this, you turn sideways and *bam*, you throw the stone with all your strength, but it has to be flat on the water. Look, I'll show you.'

I remember as though it was yesterday; he performed the perfect swing, I can still see him with terrifying clarity, it was extraordinary, almost supernatural: his stone hovered for an eternity over the water, skipping six, seven, eight, nine times . . . Can you imagine, Chloë? Your great-grandfather's stones could walk on water.

Today, I am walking with my daughter on the beach at Cénitz in the depths of winter, twisting my ankle on the pebbles, the wind blurring my vision. The green grass is behind me, the blue ocean before me. Here I am crouching on the ground, wiping my eyes with the back of my hand. My daughter asks what I am doing hunkered on the strand like a toad. I tell her I am taking my time choosing the right stone; in fact I am trying as best I can to hide the memories trickling down my face behind the curtain of hair.

'Wh— . . . why are you crying, Papa?'

'I'm not crying. A gust of wind blew some sand into my eye . . . Hey, hey, darling . . . This is a solemn moment, pay attention, drumroll please, the time has come for me to teach you the art of the ricochet. It's something my grandfather taught me when I was your age.'

I pick up a stone, flat and perfectly round, not too heavy, grey as a cloud. Then I pretend to change my mind.

'Forget it, you wouldn't be interested. It's not like it's a Nintendo DS game.'

'Hey! I'm not a baby any more.'

'No, it's all right, forget it, you'll only be bored . . .'

'What's a ricochet? Come on, Papa, teach me, pleaaaase!'

'Are you sure you want me to pass on the

secrets of your great-grandfather? We could go back and watch the *Hannah Montana* DVD for the eight thousandth time if you prefer.'

'Ha ha, very funny. Stop being mean.'

'OK, all right. Now, remember what I'm going to show you: it is possible to walk on water. Watch me carefully and you'll see what you'll see.'

Using the buck teeth she inherited from me, Chloë bites her bottom lip. We are both concentrating hard, knitting our brows. I cannot afford to fail, my daughter has a very short attention span, I know I will not get a second chance. I pivot slowly, tracing the arc of a circle, my arm straining behind me, my hand flat like an Olympic champion's. Then I uncoil, unleashing all my energy, and with a snap of my wrist I fling the stone towards the slack ocean, skimming the surface. The stone speeds towards the water and my daughter and I watch in amazement as it skips, hovering between sea and heaven, watch it ricochet, skip again, six, seven, eight times, as though it might fly forever.

*Pau, Sare, Guéthary,*
*January 2008–April 2009*

*Windows on the World*

Frédéric Beigbeder

Winner of the *Independent* Foreign Fiction Prize, this is a daring, moving fictional account of the last moments of a father and his two sons atop the World Trade Centre on September 11.

'The only way to know what took place in the restaurant on the 107th Floor of the North Tower, World Trade Center on September 11th 2001 is to invent it.'

Weaving together fact and fiction, empathy and dark humour, autobiography and intellect, *Windows on the World* dares to confront the terrifying image that has come to define our world, the image onto which we project our fears, our compassion, our anger, our incomprehension.

Beigbeder is a fierce, furious, infuriating chronicler of human iniquity and human suffering, and this book is a controversial, yet surprisingly humane attempt to depict the most awful event of recent memory.

## *Holiday in a Coma & Love Lasts Three Years: Two Novels*

## Frédéric Beigbeder

One night in a Parisian nightclub and the aftermath of a marriage provide the basis for these two novels about Beigbeder's alter-ego, Marc Marronnier.

In *Holiday in a Coma*, Marc Marronnier, a shallow, superficial, rich Parisian who works as an advertising executive, is invited by his old friend to the opening of a new nightclub. Taking place over a single unforgettable night, the novel documents everything from the pit-bull bouncer on the door, to the drugs, cocktails and wannabes who frequent the club, and Marc's attempts to seduce a catwalk model (*any* catwalk model).

In *Love Lasts Three Years*, Marc Marronnier has just been divorced and – shallow opportunist that he is – has decided to write a book about it. He has a theory that love lasts no more than three years, and here – recounting the highs and lows of his marriage and taking us through brash nightclubs, vain-glorious offices and soulless designer apartments – he brings to bear the theoretical and the empirical to prove his point.